IM PRESS

Ksenia Kirillova

Fairy Tales
for Refugees

БОСТОН · **2024** · BOSTON

KSENIA KIRILLOVA. *Fairy Tales for Refugees*

Translated from Russian by K.Kirillova
Editing and proofreading by Maria Bloshteyn

ISBN 978-1960533630 (pbk)

Published by M·GRAPHICS | BOSTON, MA
    ✉ mgraphics.books@gmail.com
    💻 mgraphics-books.com

Book Design by M·GRAPHICS © 2024
Cover Design byAnastasiya Kondratyeva © 2024

Printed in the U.S.A.

Contents

Rain elves live in constant anxiety and fear that their new haven might evaporate in the blink of an eye. An unhappy ghost lingers, trapped within the crumbling ruins of an estate where he was once happy, unable to escape. A delicate snowflake stands ready to sacrifice herself, longing to share the fate of her fellow snowflakes.

Beautiful forest fairies, valiant gnomes, and indomitable serpent youths face the most daunting trials. Yet, through their struggles, they discover new joys and unearth profound meanings of existence within themselves. So, every reader is invited to find a glimmer of happiness, even in the face of adversity.

A Tale of the Rain Elves: Survival Mission

AS THE PRE-DAWN DARKNESS SWEPT over Nileen, she felt anxiety flood her entire being—pervasive, overpowering, and unusually intense this time. She was uncertain whether this fear originated from within herself or was pressed upon her from the outside. It permeated every inch of her existence, both inward and outward, leaving her feeling desperate, panicked, and frail. There seemed to be no escape from its suffocating grip, driving her to the brink of madness, as if the deepest horrors of the underworld had materialized and engulfed the world around her.

Her diminutive, almost translucent body quivered with tension. Instinctively, Nileen curled into a protective ball, seeking solace in the water, which yielded reluctantly beneath her slight weight, cocooning her tenderly and securely, akin to a feather bed. "I'm home. Everything is alright now," she whispered, though the longevity of this home remained uncertain, subject to the merciless incineration of the sun's rays. It was inconsequential whether it lasted a week or a month, luck permitting, until the arrival of more rain—all that mattered was the present moment, finding solace within this small haven of safety.

Yet, even these thoughts failed to sooth her. Awareness of the ephemeral and fragile nature of her surroundings loomed too large. She had never truly known a home, nor had she ever possessed one, none of her kind ever did. Nileen believed she had grown accustomed to this reality, much like the constant specter of death—not fear, but rather a palpable anticipation of its imminence and inevitability. However, as this morning starkly demonstrated, it was impossible to become accustomed to such fear.

In the encompassing darkness, Nileen couldn't even discern her own hands against the water's surface, a stark reminder of her precarious existence. Unable to endure the relentless anxiety any longer, she rose into the air above the water, gliding towards the nearly dry grass, untouched by the dew. Nileen paused, endeavoring to inhale the night's unadulterated air, not yet diluted by the dawn, before addressing the void with clarity:

"Mom, I'm scared."

The air beside her stirred imperceptibly, granting her a fleeting sense of the night's freshness.

"It's alright, my dear," her mother's voice reassured. "It's normal at your age. We've all been there, my girl."

"Will it always be like this?" Nileen implored, desperation creeping into her voice.

"No, no, no," her mother's soothing tone enveloped her. "As you grow older, you'll learn to live with this anxiety. You'll come to realize it's our greatest asset, the Creator's best gift bestowed upon us. Everything in this world, Nileen, is ordained with wisdom. What troubles you now is the essence of our survival. We would've perished long ago without this guiding fear. It's our compass, steering us away from peril, giving us foresight them, and guiding us to safety and helping us to find a new shelter in time. Those who forget it, perish."

"But I don't understand why I'm so afraid," Nileen lamented.

"You're not meant to understand yet," her mother patiently explained. "You're still too young, and therein lies nature's wisdom. Other creatures your age may be reckless, but we can't afford such luxury. Every mistake can cost us too much, which is why we're born with this fear, and why it intensifies during adolescence, safeguarding us from irreparable harm. You'll grow, and so will your anxiety. And that's alright."

"The days are so dark," Nileen murmured. "Everything is shrouded in gray, yet there's still no rain. In this grayness, I can't even see myself in the mirror. I long for even a glimmer of sunlight."

"It's certainly more enjoyable when the sun graces us with its presence," the mother's voice suddenly shifted, tinged with a steely resolve. "But one mustn't become too enthralled by it either. Remember how your father perished—as a boy, he was captivated by the sun's reflections as they sparkled and shimmered in him. Yet, he was already a grown man, an adult, considering that we already had a child by then. Do you understand what this means?"

Nileen nodded in silence. The age at which one might decide to bear a child now seemed a distant milestone to her. But they still had to survive those years!

"He was overly confident, thinking he had mastered survival to the extent he could reach the Caves unscathed—and look how it ended!" the mother continued solemnly. "Be careful, my dear."

"But I'm always trying to be careful," Nileen protested tearfully. "I'm afraid to live, to breathe, to stray from the water even for a moment!"

"Well, that's not feasible either, my dear. You wouldn't want to perish from fear, would you?" Her mother stressed the last words, as if discussing something forbidden, a notion too dreadful to think about it. Nileen shuddered involuntarily. Death by fear was the most senseless and dishonorable fate for a rain elf—a demise that brought shame upon the entire family. It was worse than simply evaporating under the sun's rays or freezing in the cold. During this dreadful demise, fear became unbearable, and the hapless elf, unable to endure the torment, shattered into a flurry of crystal splashes, literally torn apart. Nileen knew of no one who had suffered such a fate in their lineage, and the mere thought filled her with horror.

"You must undergo the Ritual," her mother reminded her with a hint of envy in her voice. "The doctor prescribed it for you twice a week. We adults can only dream of such luxury. Treasure this blessing, my girl, it's the finest gift youth can offer. Cherish it and remember it throughout your life, holding every fleeting moment dear. Wait until dawn and make your way to the Caves. But remember to return no later than noon—we'll need to seek out a new home."

"Already?" Nileen's voice trembled. "I hoped..."

"My dear, you are already able to understand," the mother's voice took on metallic undertones again. "Can't you see what's unfolding? Can't you feel the impending threat? Yes, the sun is absent these days, but observe how stifling it is, how swiftly the water evaporates! Our current dwelling may not endure till evening. It's time for us to relocate."

"I understand," Nileen whispered, but then, unable to contain herself, she spoke hurriedly through the tears: "Mom, why do all the other elves, unlike us, live without such turmoil? Sea and river elves reside in vast, secure homes, living out their days in tranquility. They are unacquainted with death or the dread of it, never wandering from place to place, embracing their element from infancy to old age! Even the lake elves possess their own permanent home. Why are we the only ones doomed to this torment?"

"Because we bear a sacred, monumental mission," her mother replied sternly. "We safeguard the water that graces the land, the water that, descending from the sky, does not flow into rivers or lakes. It's the water of small forest streams, which may dwindle at any moment—yet it quenches the thirst of creatures unable to reach the rivers. It nurtures the roots of plants, fills the clumsy human vessels. It's the same water that people offer to their dying loved ones in their final moments."

Nileen nodded quietly. Yes, she understood that their kind's habitat was the most precarious water, scattered in tiny pearls across the earth's surface: the water of raindrops on glass, small puddles, and the dew that falls every morning on the grass. Water whose lifespan was as fleeting as a breath, never sturdy enough to be a reliable foundation for the elves who dwelled within it.

"It's this very water that sustains all life forms, as without it, the seas and oceans alone wouldn't suffice to support life on our planet," the mother continued earnestly. "Since time immemorial, it's been the rain elves who've safeguarded this vital resource, and for this great honor, we're compelled to endure perpetual risk. Yes, the water we're bound to, upon which our existence hinges, is fragile and fleeting, but without our guardianship, it would vanish entirely. Can we truly allow that to occur?"

"We cannot," Nileen affirmed. In that moment, a swell of pride momentarily eclipsed even her anxiety.

"After the Ritual, consult the Sages on this matter," her mother advised. "They'll offer a far more comprehensive explanation than I ever could. But for now, you need to rest—as you know, getting into the Caves is not easy."

* * *

Nileen grasped why her loving mother couldn't conceal her envy at the mere mention of the Caves—to her, nothing could be more glorious. Yet, reaching there was difficult. The rain elves weren't accustomed to lengthy travels, resorting to teleportation even for the nearest Caves. Finding a suitable damp stone nearby, they focused mentally on the Ritual, striving to dissolve entirely, spreading across its slick surface, and then materializing as quivering droplets on the inner walls of the Caves.

Children and frail adult elves were never dispatched there—the risk of failing teleportation and failing to materialize on the cave wall loomed too large. Generally, ordinary elves could only venture into the Caves to undergo the Ritual, which was authorized solely by a doctor's prescription. In practice, doctors prescribed this solely to adolescents robust enough to endure teleportation relatively painlessly but in dire need of solace and sustenance, both physical and emotional.

Mom was right at this age, the already apprehensive rain elves completely lost their capacity to manage anxiety. Unprepared for the swift blossoming of their innate fear, they found themselves in a literal panic. It felt as though their translucent bodies were internally consumed by cold, freezing every cell like ice. A constant, vibrating anxiety either rendered them nearly immobile or impelled them toward immediate action. This torment plagued the teenagers incessantly, permeating not just the elf but seemingly the entire world around them, rendering everything hostile, not merely joyless but utterly unbearable.

However, within the Caves, everything was different. The Caves truly resembled paradise—everything was steeped in humidity! Water droplets cascaded from the majestic stalactites, loudly splashing into streams meandering along the underground tunnels. The walls dripped with water—a life-sustaining element so abundant here that Nileen felt as if she had ventured into a veritable sea or even an ocean. Unlike seas or oceans, from which rain elves were strictly forbidden, the path to the Caves was open to them during the rare moments of the Ritual.

The Ritual entailed traversing a labyrinthine network of caves. Initially, Nileen leapt with delight onto the surface of the stream coursing through the dark passages. The water buoyantly supported her diminutive frame, and immediately pushed her transparent body to the surface. Nileen glided along as if on a conveyor belt, unable to fathom the sudden lightness, bursting into uncontrollable laughter. She lay on her back, and the water, dependable and restorative, carried her amidst the granite walls before abruptly depositing her into the cave lake.

Nileen and her fellow elves, holding their breath, observed as the Cave began to radiate with a phosphorescent glow, and greenish sparkling stalactites, elongated like arrows, rushed with their tips straight toward them. Delicately sculpted, resembling Christmas ornaments, they reflected the green and golden hues emanating from nowhere, casting shimmering reflections across the water. The water itself seemed to glow from within, like molten lava, and Nileen, laughing, immersed herself in its tranquil golden sheen. She knew the water wouldn't scorch her; it would remain refreshingly cool.

Mesmerized, Nileen watched as a luminous radiance poured into her from the water's surface, causing her entire being to sparkle, shimmer, and refract the ineffable beauty of the Cave. Like an enchanted forest unfurling its branches, the underground grotto blossomed before her eyes in vivid yellow, green, and reddish hues, revealing patterns on the rocks, and rivaling the delicacy and beauty of frost patterns on glass.

Now, Nileen saw herself more vividly than ever—she was entirely composed of light. It danced upon the water's surface, contrasting sharply with the surrounding black shadows that penetrated the lake's depths. Unlike sunlight, these illuminations posed no threat to her. They didn't scorch her or threaten to erase her existence at any moment; instead, they imbued her with vigor and elation.

A sensation of security, so profound and nearly unfamiliar, swept Nileen away to a realm of celestial bliss beyond consciousness. Drifting upon the water, she bathed in light and shadow, while resonating drops continued to descend from above, as though reminding her that the entire world was now safe and healing—from earth to sky. As the cave came to an end and the subterranean passage resumed, light yielded to darkness, then to glimpses of timid rays that somehow miraculously penetrated from the surface. The water held varying sensations throughout: in some places, it exuded a sense of dampness; in others, it sprawled like a majestic force; and in yet others, it surged like a wild stream—playful, irrepressible, audacious...

Courage was fostered within these Caves: a total absence of fear, a celebration of life, and a yearning to live! Suddenly, Nileen spotted a striking elf nearby—tall, ablaze with internal radiance, much like herself. Amidst the cave's reflections, he appeared particularly bold to her - exquisitely audacious. There was something heroic in his cocky profile, in his almost flawlessly proportioned physique, despite his youth, and suddenly Nileen felt an overwhelming desire to fly to him and kiss him passionately. Despite the unusual surge of courage, she managed to restrain herself. Of course, thoughts of kissing were out of the question, and the issue wasn't about sanctimonious morality. As always, all limitations stemmed purely from concerns about safety.

Physical intimacy among the rain elves manifested in merging into a single stream, fervent and impassioned. With adequate strength, another tiny stream could crystallize from this union—their joint child. Inexperienced teenagers, unfamiliar with properly harnessing either their strength or vulnerability, might simply perish after such merging, unable to muster the strength to reconstitute themselves as separate, whole beings. The torrent of passion could simply wash them away, and hence such intimacy could spell doom for lovers.

Only adult elves capable of managing their emotions chose to have children. This vulnerability, the inability to surrender to love without fear was also their retribution for their grand mission. Nileen often pondered, whether the rain elves would fail to be born from the heaviest downpours and floods, their race would inevitably perish in such conditions.

Nileen noticed the unfamiliar elf also observing her and hoped he remembered: they wouldn't be able to get close for a long while. Nevertheless, no one could forbid them from being friends—merely friends, innocently and purely, meticulously adhering to all safety protocols. He likely resided nearby—typically, elves from the same city were summoned to undergo the Ritual on the same designated day. The thought of potentially becoming friends with him buoyed Nileen's spirits once more. She began to envision how, perhaps, they would spend years together and then, upon reaching adulthood, navigate all challenges side by side, surely enduring until they reached the cherished Caves.

It seemed unbelievable to Nileen that within these Caves, within these incomprehensible, heavenly Caves, elves could live so effortlessly—just like herself, differing only in age. Only those exceptional elves who reached a hundred years of age were permitted to dwell permanently within the Caves. Nileen found it incredibly challenging to envision living for so long in their world fraught with dangers, inundated with anxiety. It was no wonder they were referred to as the Sages—unmatched masters of survival, those who could fully fulfill the rain elves' grand mission until the end. Yet they coped, and then retired to a well-deserved rest, where fear and demise were unknown. Here, within the ancient Caves, the Sages lived on endlessly...

For everyone else, access was granted solely for the Ritual, and Nileen believed there was wisdom in this: to behold this paradise as a child. Not only did it bolster resilience and fortitude, but it also infused life with purpose. No, she wouldn't perpetually exist in eternal fear, fretting over her future; she wouldn't forever wander amidst new bodies of water, yearning for refuge and striving to relocate before the next home evaporated with her. After enduring all of this, she would eventually find her place here. She would surely prevail, she would survive, because now she witnessed firsthand the example of real elves who had attained their happiness!

* * *

The ritual concluded, and Nileen nearly forgot the question she had long yearned to pose to the Sages. Now, fueled by a surge of recklessness, her mind began to operate with remarkable agility, and Nileen herself marveled at the clarity of her thoughts and the unexpected boldness of her inquiries.

"Forgive me, I've been eager to inquire for quite some time," she addressed the venerable elf with a fluttering heart. "My mother told me that we have a unique mission—we are the guardians of the water that sustains all life, and thus we endure all our tribulations."

"Your mother is absolutely right," the elf nodded solemnly.

"But I'd like to clarify how exactly do we guard it?" Nileen asked, her words stumbling. "I mean, we don't undertake anything special for this. We have an unwavering rule: if our habitation is drying up, and we have no recourse but to sacrifice ourselves, to dissolve within it without a trace and thereby prolong its existence, we should, under no circumstances, do so. We must relinquish our home yet preserve ourselves and seek out a new refuge."

Nileen fell momentarily silent, still grappling with her new-found courage.

"I can't help but wonder: we change residences so frequently in our lives, yet each new one inevitably dries up," she continued more confidently. "We take no action to preserve it; on the contrary, we draw sustenance and vigor from it. But if these reservoirs still deplete, if we are unable to aid them in any manner, then what is our purpose? If we serve no function, why don't we dwell in rivers or lakes and lead an ordinary, happy life, like all other elves, while the terrestrial waters disappear and appear again without our involvement?"

"How could such thoughts enter your mind!" the Sage exclaimed in horror. "Since time immemorial, the world has relied upon the elves! Only our presence sustains life within it. We needn't undertake any action for this, we need only exist. Our mission is inherently to survive, and that alone is sacred, our lives are sacred! Each element in this world is safeguarded by our presence!" he declared passionately, then, lowering his voice, he added:

"Do you understand the consequences for those who dare venture into lakes or rivers? It is a shameful death in the desert beneath the scorching sun, devoid of water, ostracized by their kin. This is not mere desertion—it is a betrayal of our mission; it is the destruction of the foundations of the universe! Never forget who you are and where you belong," he concluded solemnly.

"Of course," Nileen murmured, nodding. She fluttered towards the Cave's exit and spotted the unfamiliar elf whom she had observed during the Ritual. Under the weight of the Sage's words, she had entirely forgotten about him, yet it seemed as though he had been awaiting her all along and smiled—quite approvingly, as it appeared to her.

"Shall we go together?" he invited, pressing himself against the wall.

"Let's go," she nodded, spreading out onto the stone beside him. "Where would you like to appear?"

"At the old tower in the historical quarter of the city," he promptly responded. "There was a pipe burst this morning, water is gushing everywhere, all the stones around are splashed completely."

"Fantastic!" Nileen exclaimed. "Let's hurry!"

Finally melding into the damp cave wall, they were swiftly carried by the surge of energy from the Ritual into the city, arriving amidst a sparkling fountain of spray from the ruptured pipe.

"How marvelous, how wonderful!" Nileen cried, soaring into the sky. The sun bathed everything in radiant light, and the elf basked in its warmth with delight. Strengthened by the Ritual, she felt no fear at the scattering of solar sparks, especially with so much saving water nearby. Laughing, she marveled at her newfound carefreeness as if the night's paralyzing fear had never occurred.

"Where do you live?" Nileen inquired of the elf, finally descending to the ground.

"Right here," he chuckled, gesturing toward the broken pipe.

"But that's very risky!" Nileen began to regain her customary caution. "This pipe could be repaired at any moment, and then all the water will dry up rapidly."

"Well, it would dry out just the same in any other place," the elf laughed in response.

"Yes," murmured the bewildered Nileen, "but elsewhere, at least there's hope, whereas here we know for certain it has no other source."

"In simpler terms, it's easier for us to delude ourselves elsewhere," the elf continued. "But how can self-deception aid our survival?"

Nileen was utterly perplexed. She no longer knew whether he was jesting or speaking earnestly.

"I overheard your query to the Sage," her newfound acquaintance continued. "And you know, I think you're right. Perhaps we once had a mission to preserve all living things, but I have a sense that we lost it long ago."

"But the Sage said..." Nileen began to argue.

"After all, flower elves are actually unable to preserve the flowers in which they live. Every autumn they perish alongside them, only to be reborn in spring with the first grass," he continued, paying little heed to her words. "Unlike us, they are too carefree and fail to comprehend death, which is understandable—they have no chance of survival regardless. Though theoretically, since they cannot save their flowers, they could relocate to warmer climes where cold never encroaches and dwell there forever. It seems none of us elves are fulfilling our original mission anymore, and we suffer out of habit, entirely in vain. Yet, it's impossible to verify, even the Sages cannot discern the truth. No one dares to break the taboo and depart, and if we stay put, we'll never know how the surface world fares without us."

"So, what should we do now?" Nileen inquired, confused.

"Nothing," the elf laughed again. "Just live, try to enjoy life. And perhaps, don't be overly fearful, for the world may not be as it seems."

"No," Nileen protested. "The threats are very real, and elves do perish from them. My father died from sun exposure. Would you claim that's also an outdated legend?"

"Well," the elf responded diplomatically. "Of course, caution is necessary. I'm not suggesting otherwise. But it's crucial not to let fear consume you to the point of death."

"I've heard this before, but I've never seen a single elf perish from fear," Nileen admitted.

"My father," the young elf replied, unexpectedly solemn. "Perhaps I'm foolish for telling you this. It's not customary to discuss such matters, but my father died of fear..."

Nileen stared at him, incredulous. This elf, brave to the point of recklessness, came from a family marked by disgraceful lineage? His father, his own flesh and blood, was a feeble coward who fell to pieces, failing to utilize the very instinct bestowed upon him to fulfill their unique mission? Was she standing before the son of a coward?

"What, are you going to shun me now?" the elf asked bitterly. "Do you think I'm the only one? It's just not spoken of, but in truth, many elves perish from fear. Consider it—who would confess to such a thing? Fear was once heralded as the greatest virtue—perhaps it was. But it seems now it does more harm than good."

"What are you saying?" Nileen felt a wave of dizziness. She sat upon the water, yet even its soothing coolness did not bring the long-awaited relief.

"Don't dwell on it," the elf attempted to comfort her. "Just avoid excessive fear, any adult will tell you that."

"Yes, my mother said the same," Nileen nodded, still reeling. "By the way, what's your name?"

"Vincent," the elf smiled again, a beam of sunlight passing over his face and infusing it with an uncommon radiance.

"Vincent," Nileen whispered admiringly. "A noble name. Do you hail from an ancient lineage?"

"Somewhat," he laughed softly. "If you wish, we could spend more time together. Where do you live?"

"I'm not sure," Nileen hesitated. "We must relocate today; our dwelling is drying out... Oh dear," she realized. "It's nearing noon, I must return. We need to search for a new home."

"Of course," Vincent nodded seriously. "Ah, the repair truck has arrived. Soon they'll destroy my beautiful home, so it appears we're kindred sufferers. Don't fear, I'll find you, wherever you may be. Good luck with your resettlement!"

"And you," Nileen replied.

"Have no worries, these fellows have several hours of work ahead," Vincent waved dismissively.

"Regardless, don't delay in finding a new home," Nileen requested, then added unexpectedly to herself, "It would be very hard for me if something were to happen to you."

* * *

All subsequent days and weeks blended together for Nileen into a seamless stream of happiness. Not a day passed without her seeing Vincent. The fountain in the main square of the city finally began to flow, and they whiled away countless hours each day amidst its refreshing spray. Nileen's anxiety didn't vanish entirely, but it dulled somewhat, and the young elf gradually learned to manage it. Mornings remained the toughest, as fear gripped her upon waking, but as she learned to rein it in, she found herself eagerly anticipating happiness—happiness embodied in the form of Vincent.

This routine persisted until one day when he suddenly proposed, "Nileen, wouldn't you like to visit the Caves?"

"I would," she sighed, "but we've already attended the Ritual twice this week, and the next opportunity is a week away."

"No, that's not what I meant," Vincent interjected. "I'm suggesting a stroll in the Caves."

"That's impossible!" Nileen exclaimed, regarding him as if he were insane. "No one will grant us access there."

"We can gain entry through acquaintances," he countered. "Through connections, as humans say. I happen to know several Sages quite closely."

"Did you know them before they retreated to the Caves?" Nileen began to guess.

"Exactly," Vincent affirmed. "They're all from aristocratic families, residents of the Mists." Seeing her confusion, he added, "Are you really so naive as to believe that ordinary rain elves can live for a century?"

Nileen fell into a despondent silence. Why had she never considered this before? Surviving in misty regions was undoubtedly easier than in arid ones, but only members of ancient aristocratic lines were permitted to settle there. So it was they who became the Sages? It dawned on Nileen belatedly that she and her peers had no personal connections to any of the Sages prior to their retreat to the Caves. Did that mean elves outside their circle had no chance of survival?

"Our family resided in the Mists," Vincent divulged. "We were expelled after my father's death—his disgrace brought shame upon us. We lived well there until an unusually dry year when the fogs failed to materialize for months. Unprepared, many perished, including my parents. Not all succumbed to fear, but such instances occurred. In prosperous times, we never learned to manage our anxiety, so we were ill-equipped for it."

"Are you an orphan?" Nileen inquired sympathetically. He nodded.

"Mother couldn't foresee that the dew would vanish from the grass. Those who survived eventually relocated to the Caves. I had agreed to go there today, but if you wish, we can go together."

Nileen couldn't believe such fortune—a chance to visit the Caves, the coveted Caves, without restriction! Speechless, she merely nodded. They soared to the nearest rock, and Nileen, closing her eyes, surrendered to the anticipation of impending bliss. Moments later, they stood within the unusually quiet, deserted Caves.

"Vincent, are you alone?" Nileen heard a Sage's voice.

"With a friend," he replied. "She's trustworthy."

"I hope so," the Sage muttered. "I won't disturb you, just behave yourselves," he cautioned before vanishing into the tunnel.

In the cavern's depths where Vincent and Nileen found themselves, no familiar stream flowed, yet healing humidity enveloped them, inducing a serene relaxation in every cell. Holding her breath, Nileen followed Vincent further into the shimmering depths.

"I don't think I've ever been here," she whispered.

"Correct," Vincent confirmed. "The Ritual isn't conducted in this particular spot."

Nileen quivered with excitement. A place where the Ritual wasn't conducted, accessible only to the Sages themselves! Or perhaps she was merely dreaming? In the flickering greenish light, walls adorned with water droplets shimmered. Nileen reverently touched them, feeling the rough lines beneath her fingertips.

"Vincent, what is this?" she asked in a hushed tone.

" Wait a minute," he replied, deftly catching the phosphorus light's reflection and directing it onto Nileen's hand. Writing emerged on the cold stone—rock paintings, almost faded by time and water, yet still visible on the granite surface.

"Wow!" Vincent whistled. "Looks like you've stumbled upon an ancient relic."

Nileen scrutinized the drawing. It depicted rain elves encircling a small oval pond, hands joined, each with a stream of water gushing from their chests like miniature fountains. Though the drawing remained still, Nileen felt as if the reservoir before her eyes filled and expanded, transforming into a small lake.

"Well, this is..." Nileen breathed out, unable to finish.

"I suspected as much," Vincent said softly, his voice unusually tinged with confusion. "I guessed, but I never imagined I'd be so right! This..." He trailed off, the unspoken understanding passing between them: the ancient rock painting depicted a long-forgotten ritual, evidence of how rain elves once nurtured the bodies of water near their habitats.

"The Sage said we just need to exist," Nileen whispered finally. "But here, it's clear that it wasn't always so. We used to share our water with the earth. Have the laws of the universe changed, or have we?"

"And then the world learned to manage without us," Vincent finished for her.

"But if that's the case, can't we safely return to the rivers and lakes?" Nileen asked hopefully.

Vincent sighed, addressing her gently, as if to a child.

"Nileen, what rivers? Do you understand the consequences? We've discussed this before: our hypothesis can't be proven, and this painting alone isn't evidence. We can't be certain if water will persist on land after we depart. The only way to know is if all, do you hear, all rain elves head to the seas and lakes. But even if one remains on the surface, it could be said that water persists because of him. Understand, no matter how convincing our theories may be, breaking the ban is unthinkable. Most elves won't agree. Even if our hypothesis is correct, it remains unprovable."

"But it shouldn't be this way!" Nileen objected, her voice nearing tears. "Perhaps everything changed long ago, and we've been dying senselessly without even knowing it! And despite our caution, we can't even reach the Caves, reserved only for aristocrats. What's the point of living then?"

"For ourselves," Vincent replied softly. "For each other. For every moment we share together."

Nileen nodded silently, wiping away her tears, and leaned into his shoulder.

The world transformed for her that day. It appeared different—not just unsettling, but also devoid of color, and even the Ritual failed to alleviate this huelessness. The water's current, as ever, whisked Nileen through the cherished tunnels and deposited her into the Cave aglow with lights. Nileen touched the gold on the surface of the underwater lake indifferently and felt that she did not want to dive into it.

She still spent time with Vincent, but an awareness of life's futility and the inevitability of death stirred within her a strange, reckless carelessness that sometimes even alarmed him. Increasingly, they ventured farther from the city, from their homes, wandering through forsaken meadows and desolate lands, gaining strength from the occasional streams stumbled on amid the grass.

Once, on the city's outskirts, they glimpsed cars—large and strikingly similar to the one that had fixed a pipe, destroying

Vincent's home on the day they met. This time, however, no pipe was in sight. Upon closer inspection, the elves observed people swarming around the wreckage of a massive apartment complex. Nileen had never witnessed such a colossal structure collapse like a house of cards. Almost echoing her thoughts, Vincent remarked:

"This happens to people sometimes. I believe they call it a gas explosion, foundation erosion, or something of the sort. Regardless, we must depart. Such locales typically experience heightened dryness or, worse, actual fire."

"But I sense the water," Nileen insisted stubbornly, darting towards the gap amidst the beams protruding from the mound of rubble and concrete. Vincent hurried after her, attempting to restrain her, but Nileen had already slipped into the cramped space and vanished into darkness. Frustrated, Vincent followed suit. Crushed by concrete slabs, a still living girl lay on the floor covered with a layer of dust. As they drew closer, she emitted a groan, as though sensing a presence nearby. Fire was approaching her—a long, advancing tongue of flame. Only a small puddle stood between the child and peril.

"Nileen, we must depart; we cannot aid her," Vincent implored. "Remember our cardinal rule—to survive at any cost. This puddle won't last. Let's drink from it, gather our strength for the journey home, and leave."

Nileen remained silent, fixating on the girl. The child couldn't see or hear them, yet Nileen stubbornly believed she was attentive to their exchange. With effort, the girl extricated one hand from beneath the rubble, extending it in a futile attempt to scoop water.

"I'm dying," she whispered, barely audible. "Mom, where are you? I'm dying..."

Nileen hovered at the edge of the puddle, suspended over its surface—warm from the encroaching fire, yet still comforting, familiar, and soothing.

"Drink!" Vincent's whisper brushed against her ear.

Nileen knelt by the water's edge, her hand pressed against her chest where her tiny elven heart pulsed. With closed eyes, she recalled the Caves, where a stream of water carried her into a realm of wonder—an embodied paradise amidst labyrinthine tunnels and stone grottoes. As eternal anxiety slowly ebbed away, it was replaced by boundless peace, enveloping her in joy. There, she and Vincent felt with their fingers ancient lines of ancient drawings...

"I'm dying," the girl murmured.

"Everyone dies," Nileen replied in the same hushed tone. "Even the flower elves cannot preserve the blooms they inhabit; they wither each autumn along with their flowers. They simply choose not to dwell on it..."

"Nileen, what's happening to you?" Vincent's voice seemed distant, unheard amidst her inner tumult. Suddenly, her heart filled with an extraordinary, indescribable fullness, then broke through, a refreshing stream gushing like a fountain from her chest, filling a small puddle.

"What is this?" The girl extended her palm under the stream, greedily drinking from it. After a few sips, she hesitantly spoke, her voice replacing the earlier hoarse whisper, initially weak but growing stronger.

"I'm here!" she shouted into the triangular gap between the beams.

"Did you hear that?" A male voice echoed from above. "There's someone down there, I heard a child cry out. Let's hurry!"

"Nileen!" Vincent grabbed her hand, attempting to pull her away from the puddle.

"Don't interfere!" Nileen interrupted weakly. "Can't you see? I'm fulfilling our mission."

"But we've discovered there's no mission anymore!" Vincent cried out in despair. "It's all just legend, an illusion perpetuated by foolish elves clinging to ancient myths."

"Let it be so!" Nileen shouted with all her might. "Let this be only a deception, only an illusion for everyone. But only I alone determine whether it's illusion or truth in my life. Only I can decide how to live it. You see, our life depends only on us."

"I understand," Vincent whispered, embracing her like never before. The two elves intertwined, merging like streams into one, strong and unyielding. As consciousness waned, Nileen glimpsed daylight filtering through the opening above, and a man's voice shouting:

"I told you, there's a child down here! Help me, quickly! The girl is lucky, it looks like there is some kind of groundwater source or something like that. Otherwise, she might not have survived."

The rescuers swiftly removed the concrete slabs, revealing the girl.

"I saw little beings," she gasped, clinging to her savior. "Two, almost transparent. They transformed into a stream, then vanished into that stone over there."

"Of course, of course," the rescuer nodded, addressing his partner. "She must have inhaled too much dust. It's a miracle she is even alive".

Handing the child to his waiting partner, he made his way out. Accidentally stepping into the spilled puddle, he cursed, hastily retreating. The sun flooded the opening, casting golden reflections on the water's surface.

A Tale of Ghostly Happiness

"WELL, NOW IT SEEMS FINE," her mother said critically, looking her over. Adele turned and quickly glanced into the mirror—dusty, covered with whitish spots and cobwebs. Leaning against the pantry wall and not secured in any way, the mirror seemed to have merged with the wall over the years, like many other objects in their humble home. The cobwebs were left undisturbed on purpose, lest the owners, peering into the pantry, would notice the obvious dissonance—a clean mirror in their kingdom of dust and dirt. Adele considered these precautions unnecessary; the owners had not inspected the pantry for years.

"And take this pie," her mother added, handing her the treat. The pie was large, human-made, clearly stolen from the kitchen, and Adele could barely hold it in both hands. She had long known that her parents were more anxious about this meeting than she was. Her mother prepared fussily but without exerting much pressure on her, though her own worry was palpable. Her father, however, was openly pressuring her, without hiding any of his priorities.

"Look, just make a good impression on him!" he admonished his daughter. "A chance like this doesn't present itself too often. He has a whole estate, his own personal estate!"

"Not an estate, but its ruins," corrected Adele, placing the pie on a dusty chest and looking into the mirror again.

"So what?" her father inquired with surprise and, as it seemed to her, with slight indignation. "It simply cannot be any other way. But at least it is his own house! Can you even imagine this? No owners!"

Adele could not imagine such a thing. A house without owners was an almost impossible dream for any brownie. A house of their own, where they wouldn't have to constantly hide from people, live in dark closets, turn invisible at the slightest provocation, mimic furniture, or walk on tiptoe, which, by the way, didn't always work out. People still sometimes heard strange rustling in the corners, knocks in the attic, and sometimes even footsteps—light footsteps of invisible caretakers of their houses, little people who lived side by side with them often throughout their entire lives...

"I hope everything works out for you," her mother sighed and, glancing guiltily at her father, quickly added, "Because if you don't like him at all, no estate is worth it. About a hundred years ago, when the war was over, it was probably easier. How many of them were left then—empty houses!"

"What are you on about!" her father chuckled. "The empty houses after the war... God forbid such a dwelling! Do you think they stood empty for long? Some were restored, and people moved in; some were simply torn down, razed to the ground. And what could be worse than a brownie without a home?"

Adele shuddered. For a brownie, losing one's home was the greatest tragedy imaginable. Cast onto the streets, abandoned to the whims of fate without their customary support and the very essence of their existence, such brownies often lost their sanity. Eventually, they would retreat to the forests, seeking refuge with the gnomes. This was the best possible outcome, as the gnomes, being the brownies' closest kin, offered a Spartan but bearable life in their subterranean colonies. The worst fate befell those who, unable to endure the loss, succumbed to despair, drinking themselves to death and perishing on the cold, unfeeling streets.

The brownies often grumbled about their human owners, but even in her brief existence, Adele had come to grasp how inextricably bound her kind was to these people. The essence of a brownie's life was anchored in the home—a modest sanctuary of warmth and comfort, a sacred space defined by the mere outline of walls. Brownies, unpretentious by nature, adapted easily to dwelling in basements and attics. They found rest on shelves in dusty closets, managed their simple households in the mezzanine, and at night patrolled their domain with an air of proprietorship, casting envious glances at the slumbering humans.

Rarely did any brownie have the good fortune to become the rightful owner of their home. This occurred occasionally when houses were sold and a new owner could not be found right away. But, invariably, someone would eventually arrive, crossing the threshold unceremoniously and noisily, burdened with an array of possessions, suitcases, boxes, and endless utensils, often accompanied by a loud-voiced family: a grumbling wife and screaming children. They would invade the cozy home of the brownie, remodeling everything to their liking, leaving no corner, however dusty, untouched.

Only occasionally did new owners fail to appear, leaving the empty home to age, decay, and transform into an abandoned monument to antiquity. In this state, it would remain frozen for decades, gradually becoming decrepit. In the best scenario, it was surrounded by a fence, the heavy gates locked, and the house remained entirely under the brownie's control. It didn't matter that the roof was peeling, or that the light yellow masonry of the walls slowly turned green with moss. For the brownies, such a dwelling was a luxury. Most importantly, there was no need to fall silent, listening to the footsteps and voices of people, or to rush headlong into the attic or freeze in the corner of the pantry at the slightest noise. All the rooms of the abandoned house were wide open to them, obedient in their accessibility.

Such brownies, as a rule, started large families where children frolicked, unaware of the perpetual caution required when coexisting with humans. Yet Julien, from the abandoned estate on the outskirts of their town, although no longer young, remained solitary. Only recently had he laid eyes on the charming brownie Adele. Now, his chosen one was hurriedly preparing for a date, while her parents urged her not to miss such a chance under any circumstances.

It was clear, however, that her mother was overcome with mixed feelings. The thought of owning an estate burned in her motherly heart, inspiring her, while a growing sense of anxiety mingled with joyful anticipation.

"As long as there are no ghosts in that estate," she said, adjusting the folds of her daughter's dress.

"And even if there are," her father immediately interjected, "they are no obstacle to us. Only people believe that ghosts live in their former homes, but in reality, try and find one! Most often, they fly in occasionally, to scare relatives and settle scores with old enemies, then return to their hell, or wherever they reside. And even if some get stuck in the ruins of old houses, they are interested in people, not us. They have no scores to settle with us."

Adele felt uncomfortable with this conversation. Quickly, she scooped up the ill-fated pie into a large wicker basket and hurried to the exit.

* * *

With bated breath, Adele surveyed the vast estate. She had perhaps overstated it when she called it a ruin. The building was quite solid, with only the occasional wall revealing exposed bricks beneath faint traces of whitewash. Graceful columns, though etched with wrinkles of cracks, still gleamed white, supporting the empty eye sockets of the arches. The walls, punctuated by black doorways framed by exposed wooden beams, seemed wounded. Some windows were boarded with plywood, preserving the rooms almost intact: high, spacious, though dirty from the pile of construction debris on the floor.

"This is my living room," Julien said proudly, leading Adele into the brightest room. Sunlight poured in through a ragged hole in the roof, its uneven brick edges framing the blinding blue of the sky.

"Do you want to see the bedroom?" Julien asked, guiding her down a corridor pierced by streams of light pouring through the empty window sockets. The bedroom was the best preserved, and despite its dilapidation, it still felt cozy, with remnants of light wallpaper visible on the walls.

From the outside, the estate looked particularly impressive: massive walls, protruding semicircles of towers, and pointed roofs still covered with red tiles. Although much of the furniture had been plundered before the estate was fenced in, some pieces remained: old chairs by the window, a legless dusty piano with helplessly exposed keys, and an ancient fireplace—the most untouched part of the estate. The carved doors, shutters, and a dusty spiral staircase winding in a semicircle around a column and reaching upwards were still intact. To Adele, the estate seemed enormous, like a medieval castle—incomprehensible in its immensity.

"What happened to its last owners?" she asked, realizing she didn't know what else to talk about with Julien.

"I don't remember exactly," he replied indifferently. "I know that the previous owner came to this city as a youth. He was obsessed with joining the guard and serving the king, and fortunately or unfortunately for him, this dream came true. He was happy, one would assume—young, committed, serving his master faithfully and truly, and received this estate as a reward. Then one of the nobles either set him up or slandered him. They say that one high-ranking vassal of the king turned out to be a traitor and embezzler."

"And the knight exposed him?" Adele suggested.

"No, it's not that our knight rebelled against him, but for some reason this nobleman decided he knew too much and wanted to remove the witness. In short, the king believed the slander and shamefully expelled the former owner of the estate from the kingdom. The most piquant detail was that the kingdom was surrounded by hostile states, and, finding himself outside its gates, the knight was essentially handed over to the enemies," Julien continued dispassionately.

"He died?" Adele asked in a trembling voice.

"Who knows?" Julien shrugged. "I was looking after the house, not after him. It seems the ruler intended to give this estate to another knight, but then the king himself was overthrown. The city changed hands several times, and it became unsafe to live here due to unrest and famine. You probably haven't lived through anything like this yet. Many people left, and when they returned, the estate had already begun to deteriorate and was of no interest to anyone."

Adele was somewhat taken aback by the indifference in Julien's voice. She was not accustomed to hearing brownies speak of their owners so nonchalantly—even their former owners. No, brownies did not grovel before humans. They sometimes scolded humans or could be annoyed by them, but the owners invariably occupied such a significant place in a brownie's life that they evoked any emotion except indifference.

Yet Julien seemed indifferent to everything except his beautiful home, and Adele felt a pang of understanding. She was ashamed to admit it, but she found herself falling in love with the estate. That's right: not with the brownie who had invited her, but with the breath of antiquity exuded by the brick walls, the rare, orphaned furniture as if left by a receding tide, the layers of dust on the stairs—in a word, with the place itself, not its owner.

"Where did you live before, while the knight was alive?" she asked Julien.

"Like everyone else, in the attic. Do you want me to show you?" he suggested. Adele nodded.

The attic was surprisingly better preserved than the rest of the estate and, compared to the other rooms, did not look so abandoned.

"Your pie needs to be moved into the sun to warm up," Julien said belatedly, fussing about. "And now I'll pour some water. I have a stream nearby, it's beautiful!"

He hurried down, leaving Adele in the attic cluttered with old things. Covered in a layer of dust, paintings leaned against the walls in neat rows—portraits of ancient knights, removed from the living room because they were no longer needed. Adele approached one and shone a miniature flashlight on it—an obligatory device for brownies. The smooth half-profile of a handsome man appeared before her, and the young brownie couldn't help but think she would like to have such an owner.

"Yes, that's how I looked in my youth," she heard a light rustling voice in her ear.

Adele shuddered. It seemed as though a layer of dust separated from the attic wall and slowly drifted toward her; it thickened and began to take on the outline of a person—the very person from the portrait she had just seen. Her parents' words about ghosts flashed through her mind, interspersed with a multitude of other thoughts. Could he not see that she was not human? Her father had said that ghosts had no claims on brownies.

"Have you lived here before?" she asked, her voice trembling with uncertainty, belatedly realizing how foolish her question sounded. Why was she framing it in the past tense, when it was clear that he lived here and now? Or was he merely passing through, visiting this earthly refuge for a fleeting moment? But why had he chosen this exact time, coinciding with her visit? What did he want from her?

"Yes, I have," the ghost replied, his understanding evident. "And these were the happiest years of my life," he added, his voice tinged with a wistful nostalgia.

"Do you miss them?" Adele ventured, her fear slowly giving way to a cautious sympathy.

"Every minute," he murmured, drifting slowly toward the center of the attic.

"And do you often... visit these places?" Adele hesitated, struggling to find the right word. The ghost chuckled softly.

" I fear I am bound to this place—inextricably bound," he emphasized, the last word. Adele was silent, not knowing what to say. There was no pride or bitterness in his words, only a profound, unspoken sorrow.

"Can't you find peace?" she ventured, her voice barely more than a whisper.

"In a sense, life here could be called peace," the ghost replied with a bitter smile. "Or rather, I can find nothing else."

"But why?" Adele pressed on, youthful ardor flaring in her chest. "From what I understand, you were not guilty of anything—you were betrayed..."

"That is not the point, unfortunately," the ghost sighed. "You may find it surprising, young lady, but after death, the difference between betraying and being betrayed is not as great as it seemed in life." He drifted closer, settling atop an old chest, blurring it with his whitish outlines. Adele waited patiently, not daring to rush him, but when he remained silent, she finally asked:

"How did it happen that you remained on earth?"

"I chose it," the ghost answered dryly. "They say that after death, your entire life flashes before you in the most minute detail, as if it were laid out on the palm of your hand, compressed into a single, eternal present. But for some reason, that was not the case with me. I remembered only those moments in which I was happy—so vividly, more intensely than ever before, as if I were composed entirely of longing for a small fragment of my life. I regretted, and still regret, the naivety and zeal with which I pursued my goals when I believed in my king and saw a brother in every fellow guard. It seemed to me that we were fulfilling a sacred duty, so each of these men became indescribably dear to me, embodying that sacredness. My country was the greatest love of my life, and I existed only for that love. It inspired me, guided me, saved me, filled me with meaning, and gave me happiness. I was happy here in a way that I believed no one else could ever be..."

"But that is wonderful!" Adele exclaimed, captivated by his tale.

"There must have been something in my life before that time, and something after," the ghost continued. "After my expulsion from the kingdom, I didn't die immediately. I wandered through foreign lands, unwilling to become a traitor, and so I found no refuge anywhere. My memories of that time are hazy, as if seen through a veil. I realized then that the life I had known would never be the same, that what I had lost could never be reclaimed. And when I finally died..."

He paused, as if struggling to recall something, then, surrendering, admitted:

"You know, I don't even remember exactly how it happened. I remember seeing a corridor flooded with light. And suddenly, I understood that I didn't need the light or whatever awaited me beyond it. The only thing I desired was to return to the place where I was happy, to the estate the king had given me, where we would gather for wild feasts with my comrades-in-arms. And all around, like a garden, my country blossomed, and I was bound to it by the most delicate, invisible threads..."

"And you ended up here," Adele guessed, deeply moved by the tragedy that unfolded before her. Who, up in heaven, had played such a cruel joke on this unfortunate soul, granting his desperate wish and returning him to the place he cherished most—a place now ravaged by time, ruined, deserted, inhabited only by an indifferent brownie?

"Yes, here," the ghost confirmed. "In this house, where the pain of lost joy is felt most keenly, where I am forced to watch the slow decay of the remnants of my past, where nothing old and dear remains."

"But now that you've realized this, can't you leave?" Adele suggested hesitantly. "You've seen for yourself that you won't find your former happiness here, which means that nothing holds you anymore. The past can't be restored; you know that now."

"But I cannot leave!" the ghost replied, his voice filled with anguish. "I have condemned myself to an eternal hell in this cursed estate! I can't even step outside, into the yard, or take a single step beyond its walls. An invisible force binds me here, one I have come to accept. At first, I waited, hoping to see that same bright tunnel again, but now I have no more hope."

"But it can't be like this; it shouldn't be like this!" Adele whispered, unable to bear the weight of his words. "One weakness, one single mistake—does it mean it's impossible to correct it?"

"Perhaps so," the ghost murmured. "I've realized a thousand times over that I will never regain my former happiness. It seems my sentence is to remain here as long as even a single brick of this estate's foundation stands... But I'm glad you stopped by," he suddenly interrupted himself, a faint smile ghosting across his whitish lips, bluish shadows emerging on his spectral face. "It's been years since I've seen anyone here besides that tedious brownie."

"I'll try to visit you more often!" Adele offered earnestly. "But I must go now; the owner of the house is already waiting downstairs..." She hesitated, then added apologetically, "Well, I mean Julien—he thinks he's the owner."

"I know," the ghost chuckled. "I've learned many things since I passed that I never knew in life. Brownies always think they're in charge, even when they share the space with humans, don't they?" He winked at her with translucent eyelids and faded into the wall.

* * *

Weeks had slipped away since that fateful encounter, and with each passing day, Adele felt the phantom's presence weaving deeper into the fabric of her life, altering it in ways both subtle and profound. On the day of the meeting, she had eagerly recounted the experience to Julien, her words laced with fervent indignation.

"What madness, what blatant cruelty and injustice!" she exclaimed, her voice rising with passion. "I can understand when the souls of murderers are condemned to wander, unable to find peace—they bear the weight of their guilt and must atone. But this poor man—he was a victim, wronged in life and now cursed to suffer even in death. It's only natural that he mourns the happiness stolen from him so treacherously. He made a mistake and realized it too late, but now he's trapped in this house like a prisoner, suffering more than he ever would elsewhere. And I have no idea how to help him!" She finished in despair.

"He suffers because he chooses to," Julien replied, his tone clipped and unsympathetic. "He was offered a path to the light, but he refused it. He wanted to stay on his estate, and so here he is. He's a free being, after all, and responsible for his own fate. But in doing so, he hasn't just ruined his own life; he's disrupting others as well. For instance, I don't need a stray ghost haunting my house. You're concerned about him, but have you thought about what it's like for me to live with an unwanted spirit? I've bumped into him in the corridor a few times, and believe me, I would pay dearly to have him gone. But what can we do now?"

Adele sighed, but after this exchange, she found herself yearning for each new visit to Julien—for another chance to see the tormented ghost and perhaps, in some small way, ease his suffering through their conversations. And indeed, every time she returned to Julien's home, she encountered the spirit. She learned his name had been Michel, that in life he had not only been a guardsman but had also risen to a high position at court—not through deceit or intrigue, but by undertaking the king's most perilous and challenging missions.

"I never sought power or titles," Michel would explain, almost apologetically. "It all came naturally... and it was what destroyed me in the end."

As Adele listened to his tales, it was as though a portal to the past had opened before her eyes. The bare, age-stained walls seemed to transform, becoming new again, adorned with fresh wood. Furniture reappeared in the empty halls, a fire crackled in the hearth, and the rich scent of roasting meat filled the air as candles flickered to life on long banquet tables. The estate was reincarnated in those moments, reborn anew, and with it, the entire world seemed to slip back into a bygone era. She could almost see the grand royal receptions, the lavish balls where beneath the veneer of frivolity lay the deadly intrigue of palace conspiracies, where fragile human destinies could be shattered like reeds.

Michel's world captivated her, drawing her into its enchanting, almost otherworldly atmosphere. Adele, who had always lived in a modest, semi-rural home in a small town among ordinary folk, now found herself glimpsing a world far beyond the reach of most—the world of society's upper classes. Thanks to their conversations, the ghost was once more enveloped in memories that seemed to bring him a strange comfort. He often remarked that she reminded him of someone from his past, though he could never quite place who. His life before the royal guard had become a blur in his mind, compressed into a single, hazy day, stripped of meaning yet lingering just out of reach.

As Adele's bond with the ghost deepened, it stirred growing discontent in Julien. Initially, she had attempted to share with him the wondrous world Michel had revealed to her, but her stories only seemed to irritate the new owner of the estate. Sensing his displeasure, Adele began to conceal her meetings with the ghost. She would invent reasons to visit the kitchen alone or slip up to the attic under some pretext, meeting Michel in secret. He would invariably materialize from the wall, as if a layer of dust had separated itself, thickening into his familiar form.

At night, lying in her small closet-like room, Adele found sleep elusive, her thoughts consumed by the ghost. Strangely, had Michel been a living man, he likely would never have stirred such feelings in her. The place of humans in a brownie's heart consisted of a unique blend of affection and respect for boundaries, a line that seemed unthinkable to cross. But Michel was no longer human, and thus, the usual rules did not apply. This remarkable, deeply sorrowful being, whom Adele had never before encountered, penetrated her heart as effortlessly as he passed through walls—a whitish mist, clothed in the elegant form of memory and melancholy.

Adele knew that falling in love with such a creature was akin to madness. No one truly knew if the brownies possessed immortal souls. Legends were contradictory, and there were no accounts of brownie or gnome ghosts. She understood that if this were true, she would never meet Michel even after death.

To her dismay, Julien was unwilling to tolerate her infatuation with the ghost. Adele herself began to find it increasingly difficult to converse with him. What could she talk about if she couldn't speak of what mattered most to her? Julien's presence became an ever-growing burden. At first, she dismissed it as the natural awkwardness of their early acquaintance, attributing it to the lack of habit of interaction with another brownie. But she soon realized there was no point in deceiving herself—Julien was unpleasant to her, and this alone nullified any possibility of a future relationship.

Yet, the more alienated Adele felt from Julien, the more she was drawn to his estate, which in her mind had become Michel's house. She would have given anything to meet the ghost somewhere else, but they were both trapped by his tragic attachment to the estate. It was clear that such a situation couldn't last long.

"You only come here for your ghost!" Julien finally snapped one day. "Well, my house is not a place for dates with spirits. Go talk to your talking sheet somewhere else!"

"You know that's impossible!" Adele retorted angrily, only to realize she had spoken rashly. Usually calm and indifferent, Julien erupted in fury.

"So you don't even deny that you come here because you can't meet him anywhere else!" he raged. "Well, let me tell you something—you won't set foot in this house again! Get out! If he wants to talk to you so badly, let him leave my estate—I don't care how he does it. I've been dreaming of getting rid of him for a long time."

Adele's attempts to reason with Julien—pleading, negotiating, even trying to appease him—were all in vain. He remained resolute; his stance unyielding. Julien knew too well that she was indifferent to him, and now he sought his revenge—petty and cruel.

In the days following their quarrel, Adele clung to a fragile hope that a miracle might occur, that Michel's attachment to her would somehow shatter the spell that bound his tormented soul to the decaying estate. But no such miracle came—the ghost remained elusive, stubbornly absent. Desperate, Adele wandered the grounds for hours, her eyes searching the black hollows of the windows for the familiar whitish silhouette, but Michel could not be found outside the enchanted house. An emptiness began to grow within her, vast and impenetrable, mirroring the darkened windows of the forsaken estate. The "ghost of high society" had vanished from her life.

* * *

"That's how it all happened," Adele concluded her story, her voice tinged with guilt as she looked at Martin. They sat huddled in a cramped closet within a modest, somewhat shabby house. The thin walls did little to muffle the incessant wails of a child crying from the adjacent room.

"Yes, I pity the poor fellow," Martin replied, his tone laden with sympathy. "It's not really living, is it? More like a slow, agonizing torture—being forced to witness the crumbling remains of your happiness day after day."

"And now, I can't even support him," Adele added with a pained expression. "Julien doesn't want to see me. I have to break the news to my parents somehow too—they'll be so disappointed. They had such high hopes for our relationship. But I can't keep this a secret forever."

"No, you definitely can't," Martin agreed with a solemn nod. "Julien's already moved on—he's got a new girlfriend. They're inseparable, and sooner or later, the whole town will know."

Adele stiffened at the news as if someone had informed her that her friend—ghost had suddenly found a companion. "How quickly he moved on! Who is she?"

"Plump Molly," Martin replied, almost offhandedly. "You probably know her—her family lives in the shopkeeper's house.

It's obvious why she's interested in him, given his estate. You must have heard about her brother—he went off into the forest to live with the gnomes and started a family there. Don't be surprised if a whole horde of forest creatures ends up living in your ghost's manor."

"At least he won't be lonely," Adele muttered, her mind conjuring an image of plump Molly rifling through dusty portraits in the attic with all the subtlety of an invading army. The whole town knew the tale of Molly's brother—a saga that had become a local legend, as his departure for the forest had been preceded by an epic, years-long feud with the shopkeeper's cat. For reasons no one could explain, the cat had developed an intense dislike for the young brownie and had declared war on him. To his credit, the brownie had accepted the challenge with dignity, retaliating with pranks that made the cat's life miserable. He'd mix salt and pepper into the cat's milk, hide its toys in the oven, and even sneak live mice into the shopkeeper's bed—each act a testament to the cat's glaring incompetence. Naturally, the shopkeeper blamed the cat for all these mischiefs, punishing it severely with brooms and rags. Had the wily brownie not finally fled, the enraged feline might have destroyed his entire family.

Martin's own situation was hardly better, though he considered himself somewhat luckier. His owners were a large family, recently expanded by the birth of another child. With both parents working, they had hired a nanny for the baby. Unfortunately, there was no spare room for her, so the young, rather crude nanny had been given a place to sleep in the pantry, shamelessly violating the brownie's personal space. The worst part was that the nanny had a fondness for alcohol, which she indulged in whenever the parents were out. She took great pains to dilute it and disguise the smell with a bizarre concoction of perfumes and spices, but Martin, hidden away in the shadows of the pantry, saw it all. Such behavior from a nanny responsible for a small child was utterly disgraceful to him, yet there was nothing he could do about it.

Martin's only solace came from the middle daughter of the household. Unlike the adults, who had long since lost the childish ability to perceive brownies, she retained a keen sense for them. She would even leave out a saucer of milk "for the brownie"—though the new nanny would treacherously take it away more often than not. It was clear that, without even a pantry to call his own, Martin was not exactly an enviable groom. Yet, he had been Adele's closest friend since childhood, and now, he awkwardly tried to offer her comfort in the midst of her troubles with the ghost.

"Maybe Molly will manage to find common ground with him and brighten his exile in the estate?" he suggested, grasping at hope.

"I'm not sure Michel will even speak to her," Adele replied uncertainly. "He had a special way of treating me. He once told me I reminded him of someone from his past."

"Maybe that's the key," Martin said suddenly, as an idea struck him.

"What key?" Adele asked, puzzled.

"His curse," Martin explained impatiently. "Perhaps the answer lies in his past, in the part he doesn't remember. You've always said he's perfect, an innocent victim. Maybe that's true in his dealings with that nobleman, but surely there's more to his life than that one story. What if there's a dark past he's forced himself to forget—a past so painful it keeps him tethered to this world?"

"But what does that have to do with the estate?" Adele questioned, her voice tinged with doubt. "He longed to return to it more than anything. His wish was granted to the letter. There doesn't seem to be any connection to anything else."

"But that's exactly what's off," Martin insisted. "It's his past. It's not normal that he remembers so little of it, and what he does remember, he idealizes to the point of obsession. He still longs for that part of his life, doesn't he? Even though he knows he'll never find his former happiness in the estate, he's still drawn to it."

"Do you mean this longing is what's keeping him bound?" Adele began to grasp his idea, wondering why she hadn't thought of it herself.

"I'm not certain," Martin admitted, shaking his head. "But he needs to try to remember, to reevaluate something. I can't see any other way out."

"And what if there is no way out?" Adele asked anxiously. "What if his posthumous choice is irreversible?"

"In any case, we have to try to communicate our thoughts to him. He needs to attempt something, anything," Martin said with determination.

"But how can we convey that to him?" Adele asked, despair creeping into her voice. "You know Julien won't let me within a kilometer of that estate now."

"Let's say he would let me in," Martin mused aloud. "But what reason could I possibly give for showing up? He's not exactly sociable..."

"He doesn't have any hobbies," Adele began to think aloud. "He only cares about the estate, which, strictly speaking, doesn't even belong to him but to a ghost!"

"The estate," Martin repeated thoughtfully. "Wait, I think I have an idea." With that, he began rummaging through the far corner of the pantry. They were alone, taking advantage of the fact that the nanny was finally attending to her actual duties, fussing over the owners' child. After some time, Martin emerged from the shadows, dragging behind him a small table and chair, perfectly sized for a brownie.

"Children's furniture," Martin explained. "The owners bought it for their eldest son. He's already outgrown it, and the youngest won't need it for quite some time. They won't miss it anytime soon."

"And you're planning to give it to Julien?" Adele gasped in surprise.

"Give it to him?" Martin chuckled. "No, I'm thinking of exchanging it for something, as brownies traditionally do."

"But when they do notice it's gone, they'll figure everything out," Adele began to protest. "They'll find you…"

"People are always more inclined to suspect one another," Martin waved away her concerns. "It's easier for them to believe the worst of their own kind than to believe in us. Besides, it won't be for a while, and right now, we need to save your ghost."

Anxious yet hopeful, Adele waited through the day for Martin's return. When he finally came back in the evening, the results were disappointing. Despite Martin's remarkable diplomacy during his conversation with Julien and his efforts to explore every corner of the estate, the ghost never revealed himself.

"Look what I traded our furniture for," Martin said, handing Adele a small gold medallion. "Julien found it in the attic."

"Almost new furniture for just a medallion?" Adele asked in surprise.

"Open it," Martin suggested.

Adele pressed the stubborn clasp with both hands, and as the medallion swung open, she froze, speechless. Staring back at her from the tiny portrait inside was her own likeness—only it was a human, an exquisitely dressed girl from a bygone era.

"So that's who I remind him of!" she whispered in awe. "If only I knew who she was." Then, turning to Martin with sudden resolve, she declared, "I must get to that estate, no matter the cost! I need to talk to him myself."

"There might be a way," Martin said quietly. "Julien invited me to his wedding…"

"A wedding?" Adele exclaimed. "Already?"

"Yes," Martin nodded. "With that plump Molly."

"But he invited you," Adele pointed out, her brow furrowed. "How does that help me?"

"He told me I could bring my girlfriend, if I had one," Martin explained, a mischievous glint in his eye. "So, if we tell him you're my girlfriend, he won't be able to turn you away."

Adele hesitated, understanding the implications. The moment they attended the wedding together, rumors would ripple through the town. She had never intended to marry Martin, and once she left him, it would look like she had spurned him, tarnishing both their reputations.

"Make up your mind; it's just one visit," Martin urged her gently. "And you'll finally have a chance to reconcile with your Julien. You can't keep avoiding each other like this."

"Alright, I agree," Adele finally nodded, her voice firm with determination. "And thank you—thank you for everything. You have no idea how much you've helped me!"

"Well, I'm trying to help more than just you," Martin replied with a hint of condescension. "I was about to say I'm saving a human's life, but then again, he's not a human, and it's a bit late to save his life anyway. Well, you get my point," he added, a sly smile playing on his lips.

* * *

At last, the long-awaited day of Julien's wedding arrived—a day that Adele had both dreaded and yearned for with agonizing impatience. Over and over, she had replayed in her mind the possible encounter with the ghost, fearing that she might inadvertently give him false hope, tormenting his already weary soul with unnecessary memories—if, indeed, he could remember anything at all. Yet, despite her fears, she longed for this meeting as if her entire future depended on it.

Julien greeted her with a mixture of surprise and cool detachment, though not with hostility. The estate had drawn a multitude of brownies, who now roamed the empty, high-ceilinged halls with crumbling whitewash, their eyes filled with awe and a barely concealed envy. Despite the dilapidation, remnants of the estate's former grandeur peeked through the vaulted ceilings and rooms, now teeming with little people—smart, excited, and intoxicated by the unexpected freedom of existing without the presence of humans. Adele wove her way among them, mechanically squeezing between the scurrying figures, her eyes searching each room. There was the bright drawing room, the darkened bedroom with boarded-up windows, a storeroom, and finally, the longed-for attic. Someone had already been here, and more than once—it was clear from the many footprints scattered in the dust.

"Michel!" she called softly, her voice echoing timidly off the walls, prolonging the fading sounds for a split second. The ghost did not answer. Adele circled the spiral staircase in vain, peering into the sunlit air. It seemed to her that, just a little longer, and the dust, thickening, would begin to take on the form of a familiar silhouette. But it was all in vain. The air, untouched by the whitish haze, remained stubbornly transparent, revealing the intricate patterns still preserved on the ceilings.

Small figures of cheerful brownies darted about, noisily pouring flower nectar into miniature glasses—a generous gift from a family of gnomes who, as Martin had predicted, had arrived in a crowd from the forest. Martin, too, was enjoying himself, though Adele noticed out of the corner of her eye that he watched her with concern. Unable to bear the sight of others' joy, she slipped away into a back room that had once belonged to the servants. It was in the worst state of preservation, with nearly the entire back wall gone. Bold grass, like a predatory kite, had sensed the decay first and began to grow vigorously through the cracks in the floor and the remaining walls. Where people had once lived, now spring flowers bloomed, and Adele, once again, searched the courtyard that had taken shape in place of the room, hoping to find Michel.

"Hello, are you Adele?" a ringing voice suddenly called out. A translucent flower elf appeared, seemingly emerging from the ground itself, and began fluttering his wings before her face.

"Yes, I am Adele," she responded, startled, trying to recall where she might have encountered this elf before.

"I have something for you," the elf said slyly, darting about in front of her, flitting in various directions.

"Really?" Adele replied indifferently, unable to imagine what such a tiny creature could possibly have in store for her.

"A message from a ghost," the elf whispered ominously, then plunged downward like a falling star, as if frightened by his own words.

"A ghost?" Adele exclaimed, frantically turning her head in all directions, desperate not to miss a single word. "Please, tell me—what did he say? It's very important! Where is he?"

"He is not here!" the elf replied loudly. "He is not here and shall never be. He has flown away to a place far away from which no one returns."

"Truly?" Adele felt a wave of joy and incredible relief wash over her, but it was immediately tempered by a sharp, almost resentful pang of sorrow. Why hadn't he waited for her? Why hadn't he said goodbye? If he had finally managed to leave the estate, why hadn't he sought her out in the city?

" How did he leave?" Adele asked, looking at the elf flit about.

"Beautifully, beautifully he left," the elf chirped, spinning in the air. "In the dead of night, light poured down from the sky—either a beam or a shower of stars. And he soared up within that very beam."

"A glowing corridor..." Adele whispered. "And he didn't even try to find those he knew on earth?"

"He couldn't, I tell you, he couldn't!" the elf insisted, his excitement palpable. "That stream of light—it pulled him in, straight from the estate, and that was that. But before it happened, he managed to tell me that if you came here, I should definitely tell you how grateful he is to you. He said it was thanks to you that he remembered the girl he left behind because of joining the king's guard—or something like that," the elf continued, his tone suddenly sheepish. "She loved him very much, it seems, and he probably loved her too, but his dream of becoming a guard was stronger. Thanks to you, he remembered her and realized that much of his past was an illusion, an obsession," the elf concluded crisply, pronouncing complex words with difficulty.

"But he seemed so happy then!" Adele exclaimed, her confusion deepening.

"Well, I don't know how humans do it," the elf replied in a ringing voice. "All I know is that he told me his happiness was incomplete, and after your conversations, he realized that there could be another kind of happiness—greater, fuller." The elf's voice was devoid of personal understanding; he simply relayed the message with mechanical precision.

"After our conversations, he didn't seem very happy at all," Adele murmured, bewildered.

"Well, I don't understand how everything works for him," the elf replied with a hint of irritation. "I think it's very simple to be happy—just live and enjoy life. But him... I never saw him happy, but it seemed to me that, for the first time, he believed that real happiness could await him—not the kind he had, but something different, something better. That's what he wanted you to know..."

"So, we were right," Adele said quietly. "He thought the same as Martin and me. He understood the same thing, and he succeeded."

She thanked the elf and slowly made her way to the attic. Adele knew she should be happy for the ghost. Hadn't she dreamed of this moment for so many long months? But why, instead of joy, did she feel only a deep, aching melancholy? It seemed to her that one meeting, one conversation, one farewell would have allowed her to accept his departure with a quiet, even bittersweet sadness, as one accepts the inevitability of death. But now, the unrealized conversation seared her soul with the sharp pain of loss. It seemed to Adele that all the most beautiful, most magical moments of her life were entwined with the ghost, and nothing could surpass them.

She ascended to the attic and gently moved his portrait from the wall, revealing that same mesmerizing half-profile. Adele caught herself still conversing with him in her mind. She took the medallion from her pocket and imagined that she, Adele, was the girl from the past whom Michel had loved. Here he was, leaving for his dream—to serve the king faithfully and truly, and she, left behind, understood with a painful clarity that his love for his country would always outweigh his love for any one person. He was leaving for a distant world full of intrigue and danger, seeking some elusive male happiness, and she remained to wait, now and forever...

"I will wait," she whispered softly. "I will remember him, cherish every moment, every meeting. I will live with this memory, because now I know that he is happy..."

Suddenly, Adele heard footsteps. She turned to see Martin standing in the attic doorway.

"He flew away," Adele whispered, her voice carrying the weight of loss as she answered Martin's unspoken question. "We succeeded—or rather, he succeeded without us. He rethought everything, and now he's gone. He didn't even say goodbye..."

"But everything ended well," Martin offered hesitantly, trying to comfort her. "For me too, actually."

"How so?" Adele asked, forcing herself to sound interested, though her mind was still consumed with thoughts of the ghost.

"The alcoholic nanny finally quit," the brownie replied with a smug grin. "I may have slipped something into her drink, made her quite ill. But she deserved it. The master's house is no pub for her. I'm like Molly's brother, you know. One must protect what's theirs!" He paused, pleased with himself. "In the end, the mistress decided to look after the child herself, so now I have my own separate storeroom," he finished happily.

"Congratulations," Adele replied, managing a faint smile.

"Let's go downstairs—everyone's celebrating. And it would be odd if we stayed apart the whole time," Martin suggested, a touch of awkwardness in his tone.

"Yes, of course," Adele nodded, trying to discreetly tuck the medallion away, but Martin noticed and spoke with unexpected firmness.

"I think you should leave it here. It was his life, his past. Let it stay where it belongs." Seeing her hesitation, he added quietly but resolutely, "Adele, that girl isn't you. You're not a human—you're a brownie."

Adele clutched the medallion, the last tangible connection to the ghost. In her mind, she saw images of grand balls, joyous feasts, and the thrill of serving the king—a life filled with devotion and danger. Outside, spring was in full bloom, sunlight flooding the earth and piercing the abandoned estate. Her loyal friend Martin stood beside her, ready to invite her into his newly unoccupied pantry. With a heavy sigh, Adele gently placed the locket in a dusty chest. A wave of sadness swept over her again. She hadn't had the chance to say good-bye to the ghost, but now, in this small act, she was bidding him farewell: to the worry she'd felt for him, to their stolen moments, and to the world he had unveiled for her—a world that would always hold a special place in her heart, yet one that could never offer true happiness, the kind that comes from mutual love.

"Happiness can be different, happiness can be complete," she murmured, recalling the elf's words. And though she didn't yet know what form it would take, Adele suddenly felt ready to embrace this new kind of happiness.

"What are you talking about?" Martin asked.

"About life," Adele smiled softly. "You're right, let's go down. They're waiting for us."

Together, they left the attic and began descending the spiral staircase into the light-filled living room. At the foot of the stairs, a ray of sunlight—like a corridor of light—caught them, its rainbow reflections momentarily blinding. Dust motes danced in the beam like snowflakes, threatening to coalesce into a familiar silhouette at any moment...

A Tale of an Ice Heart

THE ICE CASTLE SHIMMERED WITH SUCH an unfathomable array of hues—ranging from blinding white to the deepest blue—that it was impossible to look away. Each shade refracted through billions of facets, its invisible yet perfectly smooth surfaces forming absolute geometric perfection. It felt as though the universe itself had been born here, only to shatter later into a random kaleidoscope of other colors as a cruel jest. In the endless depths of iridescent halftones, amidst the even, utterly flawless cold glow, within the impeccable precision of the lines and the clarity of each reflection, all other colors seemed not just unnecessary, but maybe even profane.

Snowflake gazed at the triangular rooftops of the towers that vanished into the infinite blue sky and at the mesmerizing ice patterns entwining each column, finding herself still in awe of the castle's beauty. Every facet, even of the smallest ice diamond, appeared as a window into another world, opening up endless labyrinths of light refraction that completely consumed her. The blinding, piercing streams of light obediently shattered against the ice, splintering into thousands of sparks, reflecting endlessly, and, absorbed by the impenetrable icy depths, merged with it, spreading across the walls in varied shades before freezing, forever tamed by the frost.

Snowflake took a step back and asked herself once more:

"Are you ready to leave this? Are you truly ready? You could stay here as long as you wish; no one would compel you to leave if you didn't want to."

She smiled at her own question and shook her head. Of course, she had already made up her mind. The flawlessly perfect ice palace was too foreign to her, too cold. She knew she would never encounter such magnificence anywhere else, yet she had an unmistakable feeling that she would not miss it too much. Something entirely different beckoned to her now.

She envisioned a forest blanketed in a snow-white cover, each branch edged with delicate carvings, drowned in snowdrifts, silent and enchanting. The snow in this forest also shimmered with countless shades, but unlike the ice castle, it wasn't a cold, impenetrable blue but a soft, warm yellowish-gold. With the gentleness of clouds, it covered the earth in an airy blanket, preserving and nourishing it until spring.

This was the snow that children rejoiced in, laughing as they shook snow from the trees, molding it into heavy, springy snowballs that flew like arrows through the forest's edge, crashing into tree bark and spreading in white blots. This was the snow that lovers gazed upon, breathless, wrapped in scarves damp from snowfall. Snowflake knew that down there she would be just one among millions, billions like her. But even such a fate irresistibly called to her, even at the cost of giving up everything she had grown accustomed to over the years.

Here, she was something else entirely—a flawless figure, carved from ice. She lived amidst this icy splendor and, like a chosen few, held the esteemed position of lady-in-waiting to the Snow Queen. She had heard countless times that many could not even dream of such happiness. Unique and chosen, she could exist in the icy chambers forever, without ever knowing the painful process of melting. She was not trampled into the dirty ground by the soles of others, nor squeezed in the warm hands of children, nor melted into water on the tearful surface of a spring crust. She could forever gaze upon the perfect beauty of the ice castle.

And yet, Snowflake dreamed of fleeting happiness—to be among her kind, if only for a brief moment, to merge with them in a sparkling unity, and to blanket the earth with shared joy. The thought of her cold, delicate form, composed of the tiniest ice crystals, acquiring the mystical ability to warm—to join in harmony with all living things and impart a sudden warmth to the budding flowers still hidden beneath the surface—seemed incredible to her. She was irresistibly drawn to her kin, to the billions of other snowflakes, to a world of joy, creation, and warmth that, for at least a few months, did not promise her a painful end.

And then, when that inevitable end finally arrived, Snowflake would face it alongside her fellow snowflakes. They would merge into a single stream, sharing a common fate. This communal existence seemed so fantastical and extraordinary that even the thought of death did not frighten her. Even if it was just for a little while, even if it was only for a fleeting moment, she would be truly happy.

But the most difficult task remained—escaping the Snow Queen. The plan that had formed in Snowflake's mind seemed daring, even cruel, but she saw no other way out.

"Are you truly ready to undertake this on your own?" the Queen asked incredulously, her eyes narrowing in suspicion. "Do you believe you can deliver the ice to the mainland?"

Snowflake nodded firmly, her voice barely a whisper as she replied, "Yes, my Queen. On the condition that you allow me to stay in the forest afterward, among my kin."

"You must be mad," the Queen replied in astonishment and looked at Snowflake piercingly; "You don't understand how incredibly fortunate you are compared to them. Their meaningless, brief existence as dust scattered on the ground cannot even begin to compare to what you have here—a life of eternal bliss in the most perfect place on earth!"

"I know all this," Snowflake murmured, looking down.

"Everyone desires what they do not possess," the Queen said with disdain. "Can you even comprehend how many would eagerly take your place?"

"Perhaps they are more deserving of it," Snowflake ventured timidly.

"Perhaps," the Queen conceded, raising an eyebrow, not bothering to argue. "In any case, I need you to complete this task. And remember: my mirror will reveal when the ice has reached its destination. Any substitution, if you've planned one, will not succeed. The piece of ice must enter the heart—there is no other way, you know that."

"I understand, Queen," Snowflake responded submissively. "I will do everything as you wish. If a person desires it, well, he has the right to obtain what they wish…"

"Then let all the wishes in the world come true!" the Queen laughed, her voice cold. "Do what you must, and you may go. But if you fail to carry out the order, you will atone for your mistake in my palace forever, and then don't even dream of gaining your freedom, do you understand?"

"Yes, Queen," Snowflake said barely audibly, nodding.

"Then go to the trolls," the Queen commanded. "They have likely received new requests by now."

Snowflake nodded once more and disappeared into the depths of the palace. The Queen watched her go in silence. "If this ungrateful fool accomplishes what I need, there is no point in keeping her," she mused. "I can find hundreds like her, and she will inevitably pay for her foolishness. After indulging her whim, this fool will melt away in a matter of months. Well, it seems that's exactly what she deserves," she concluded with vindictive satisfaction.

* * *

In the small ice outbuilding—a mere extension of the grand castle—work was in full swing. The trolls labored meticulously, sorting through the requests sent from the mainland, fully aware of the gravity of their task. A single mistake could mean disaster. Snowflake smiled to herself, recalling the naïve human legends of a little boy who, without realizing it, had shards of a magic mirror lodged in his eye and heart. Sadly, or perhaps fortunately, it was just a charming fairy tale. Snowflake knew all too well that ice was the Snow Queen's most coveted treasure—no one received it without paying a price.

To obtain this extraordinary gift—an icy heart—a person had to truly desire it. The desire had to be clear, sincere, profound, and most importantly, deserved. Only such genuinely powerful requests, forged from the fusion of mind, emotion, and will, were worthy of the trolls' attention. Their many years of experience had shown that even those who claimed to long for an icy heart were often undeserving, unable to truly accommodate the Snow Queen's gift.

This was especially true of sensitive young women who had fallen victim to all manner of cruelties, from the most brutal violence and deceit to their own unfulfilled whims. In those moments of despair, they believed themselves ready to hate the world. Enraged, unable to forgive others for their perceived happiness, they convinced themselves that they were prepared to trample over the suffering of others with the cold indifference of a murderer.

But it wasn't only young women who sought solace in a heart of ice. Wounded soldiers returning from the front, young boys beaten nearly to death by drunken fathers, abandoned old men, and disillusioned lovers—these were just a few of the many who sought the Snow Queen's mercy. Yet, they all shared a common trait—a withering pain that gave birth to a powerful illusion of heartlessness, so convincing that it seemed indistinguishable from reality.

They now wanted only one thing—to prevent unnecessary weakness, so similar to the one that once led them to tragedy. They clung to the belief that the only way to survive in this cruel world was to turn their hearts to stone, to feel no one's pain but their own, to live solely for themselves. It seemed to these victims of human malice that the entire world owed them a debt, but they quickly realized that no amount of suffering could ever fill the void within them.

Time and again the trolls answered their silent pleas, sending snowflake ladies-in-waiting to plant shards of ice into the hearts of the afflicted. The snowflakes carried out their orders faithfully, yet as soon as these embittered souls were faced with the opportunity to commit a true act, their inherent goodness would inexplicably resurface. It was as though their true nature, deeply ingrained within them, could not be extinguished. Those who had once fancied themselves monsters would suddenly, almost instinctively, perform acts of kindness, causing the precious ice shard to melt within their hearts that which had begun to come to life.

"Such requests must be rejected immediately," the Queen would admonish, casting a sharp glance toward the trolls. "Answering them is a waste of ice. Only those who have truly made their choice, who are ready to prove it through action, and who need just the slightest nudge to snuff out the last remnants of pity, are worthy of an icy heart. By the time they seek us, their hearts should already be freezing on their own—we merely assist in completing this mystical process."

It took a masterful skill to distinguish true determination from mere illusion. Often, the victims believed so sincerely in their capacity to change beyond recognition that it was nearly impossible to suspect them of deception. Even the wisest of trolls, with centuries of experience, would sometimes hesitate, unsure whether to respond to yet another request. This was one of those times.

"The situation is uncertain," the chief troll reported with gravity to the Snow Queen. "The subject's name is Jacqueline. She lived in a small village caught in the crossfire of two warring kingdoms. Recently, one of them managed to reclaim the territory. The battles were fierce, as if the very earth had ignited from within. The village was reduced to ashes, and the victorious army, drunk on bloodlust, slaughtered entire families. Jacqueline lost everything—her home, her family."

"A common tale," the Queen interjected coldly. "That, in itself, is meaningless."

"Undoubtedly, Your Majesty," the troll agreed, unperturbed. "But that is merely the beginning. Jacqueline has concluded that evil and violence are the true rulers of this world, and that the only way to survive is to become a cold-blooded wretch herself, especially since she has nothing left to love or protect."

"They all reach the same conclusion," the Queen responded with a trace of disdain. "But almost none of these poor souls can truly act on it."

"Wait, Queen," the troll dared to continue. "Jacqueline has already begun to put her beliefs into practice. She chose to go to the very kingdom that destroyed her village, thinking it would be easier to exploit them, to treat them as less than human— just as they had treated her loved ones. But living among them, she learned to lie, to conceal her feelings, to pretend and deceive. She adapted to life among her enemies, reaping benefits while trampling on the memory of her family within her soul."

"That is promising but hardly sufficient," the Queen mused. "In the end, the people of that kingdom are no different from any others. She has merely adapted to survive among them, hiding her true thoughts. Do you know how many people do the same out of fear? That doesn't make them worthy of an icy heart."

"You are absolutely right, Your Majesty!" the troll responded with obsequious fervor. "Of course, not everyone. But Jacqueline has gone further. She secured a position as a servant in a wealthy household, and the owner of the house clearly had his eye on her. He is married, with a large family and children, and Jacqueline feels nothing but disgust for him. Yet she is prepared to respond to his advances, to destroy his family as an act of vengeance against those who wronged her, and to compensate for all she has lost. His wealth is all that matters to her now. The only thing she needs to fully commit to her path is a small piece of ice."

"You say she has already begun to act?" the Queen inquired thoughtfully.

"Yes, Your Majesty," the troll nodded. "She has settled into his household and started flirting with him. Given her life in their kingdom, it seems to me that she has lost herself completely. She has played the role too long, immersed herself too deeply in a life foreign to her to ever return to her former self. While her surviving kin wander in poverty and fear, she enjoys relative comfort, currying favor with their oppressors. We believe that if we assist her, she will continue down this path and ultimately become a true monster."

"Well, that does sound promising," the Queen smiled, a glint of satisfaction in her eyes. "And it just so happens that I have a lady-in-waiting ready to deliver the ice. Very well, let us take a chance on your Jacqueline," she agreed, her tone gracious.

Upon hearing of the upcoming mission, Snowflake shuddered. She had never liked the task of delivering ice, but it was the only way to reach the mainland—a place where eternal ice did not reign, and snow lingered for just a few months. Moreover, she believed that every wish on earth deserved to be granted. If someone found it easier to live with an icy heart, who was she to deny them?

For Snowflake herself, for example, life in the wider world, among people and animals, in those fleeting snows that brought joy to all living things, seemed infinitely more bearable. She couldn't quite explain why she felt such a strong pull toward that world, or why, with each passing day, the magnificent ice palace felt increasingly foreign to her—painfully so, repulsive in its cold perfection. Who, if not she, could understand the profound loneliness, the unbearable heaviness of a life where the heart withered in sorrow and exile? So why not ease the heartache of those who had made their choice and would inevitably follow it?

And yet, something about Jacqueline's story gnawed at Snowflake. She couldn't shake the feeling of pity for the unfortunate girl, and deep down, she struggled to believe that Jacqueline had truly changed so much that her warm, beating heart could accommodate a shard of ice—a shard that would bind her to eternal cold. Snowflake shook her head, banishing these unwelcome thoughts, and reminded herself once more: "This is your last chance." Everyone had the right to pursue their choice if they had truly made it, and so she would help

Jacqueline in her decision. In doing so, she would fulfill her own choice—to leave the ice castle forever.

* * *

As evening settled slowly over the small town, the narrow streets, covered with snow and hemmed in by ancient stone walls, began to darken with the long shadows cast by the retreating sun. Inside the house, a fire blazed in the hearth, casting a deceptive warmth that filled the living room with a false sense of comfort. The nanny, dressed in a vibrant apron, bustled about with the master's youngest son, a chubby little boy who had not yet learned to speak. His little hands reached out eagerly, trying to grasp the golden curls that framed the nanny's face.

Jacqueline stood apart, watching this scene with a simmering fury churning within her. The sight of their tranquil, oblivious contentment felt like an affront to her. It mocked her with its innocence, its ignorance of the deep sorrow, the unbearable pain of loss, and the gnawing fear that had consumed her far more than any hunger or poverty could. This feeling of hatred was all the stronger, the more problems the nanny of the master's children created for her. She saw the nanny's sharp eyes take note of the count's attentions to her, and Jacqueline knew that it would not be long before the mistress was informed of the flirtations exchanged in her absence.

This knowledge only fueled her anger, which had become her secret sustenance. Like the molten lava seething beneath the surface of a dormant volcano, her hatred remained hidden, its fire burning quietly within her heart, concealed from the world. Yet, in moments like these, Jacqueline feared that the inferno raging within her might betray her, flaring up in her eyes and revealing the depths of her true nature. She clung to her pain like a lifeline, finding a perverse joy in the cold detachment it birthed within her.

Secrecy and indifference—these twin shields gave her a sense of security, protecting her from the threat of new wounds like the ancient walls of a city fortress. She had resolved never to lose anyone again, for she would allow no one close enough to her to matter. Never again would everything she loved collapse before her eyes because she would no longer allow herself to love...

As the nanny glanced up from the child, her eyes briefly met Jacqueline's with a strange, knowing look, as if she had somehow glimpsed the dark thoughts swirling in her mind. Startled, Jacqueline quickly averted her gaze, and the nanny, leaving the child on the opulent oriental carpet—a trophy from one of the count's military campaigns—hastily left the room.

In that instant, a wild thought sliced through Jacqueline's consciousness, sharp as lightning. The hatred that had long simmered within her suddenly coalesced into a clear, flawlessly precise combination. With a swift glance at the door of the count's study, Jacqueline let out a piercing scream and rushed toward the unsuspecting child. She scooped him up in her arms, and without a moment's hesitation, she hurled herself headlong against the wall.

"Careful, don't!" she shrieked, her voice piercing the air right beside the boy's ear. Her anxiety spilled over into the child, who began to sob, struggling to free himself from her cold hands. The count burst from his office at her cry, his face pale with alarm. Jacqueline, her breath catching in her throat, spoke quickly, her words tumbling out in a rush of almost genuine fear.

"Forgive the noise, Your Excellency. Maria left the child too close to the fireplace, and he reached out toward the flames. I barely grabbed him in time—just a second more, and he could have caught fire himself! The blaze is so strong!"

The child wailed louder, unable to explain to his father the truth—that nothing of the sort had happened.

"You saved my son's life!" the count exhaled with relief. "And Maria... that incompetent fool! I'll dismiss her this instant! Imagine such negligence—it nearly cost him his life!"

He snatched the child from Jacqueline's arms and handed him to the mother, who had rushed in, her face stricken with worry. Without another word, the count stormed out, the door slamming shut behind him. Jacqueline remained in the center of the room, but instead of the triumph she had anticipated, a sharp pang of conscience cut through her. It was a searing, knife-like pain that pierced her heart, far more intense than the flame of hatred which had once fueled her. It burned through her veins, dried out her lungs, constricted her breath, and spread weakness throughout the body. Then, a wave of nausea and fear swept over her, so dizzying that she instinctively chased after the count, desperate to stop him.

Suddenly something caught her eye—a strange shadow in the window of the living room. Jacqueline pressed her face to the glass, bewildered. The light from the house cast iridescent reflections on the snow outside, and there, on the shimmering white blanket, stood a delicate figure in a gown that seemed to be carved from frost patterns. The figure's skin appeared bluish in the twilight, a blend of icy blues and whites. The ice girl lifted her large, glistening eyes to Jacqueline, and at that moment, she felt utterly powerless to resist the gaze. Drawn by an inexplicable force, she threw a light fur coat over her shoulders and ran out onto the snowy porch.

"Who are you?" she whispered into the cold air. For a brief moment, she felt the innocent belief in miracles return to her, and in the face of this magical apparition, her earlier cruelty towards the nanny seemed even more vile.

"I've brought you something," the ice figure said, hesitating slightly.

"What?" Jacqueline asked, though fear tinged her voice, as if she dreaded the answer.

"Something you've longed for, something that will ease your life," the snow girl replied, a trace of uncertainty in her voice. "It's a piece of ice for your heart."

"Ice?" Jacqueline echoed, the words not quite registering at first. Then, as the meaning sank in, a wild eagerness overtook her.

"A piece of ice?" she cried out, her voice trembling with excitement. "Then give it to me quickly! This means I'll never feel the pain I felt today again! I'll be free to do whatever I wish, without ever suffering for it."

Her eyes sparkled with a desperate fervor, as if reflecting the snowflakes scattered around her. Jacqueline rushed toward the ice figure, seeing in it her salvation. At last, she would obtain the coveted fragment, endure the final sting in her heart, and then be enveloped forever in serene, icy calm. But Snowflake, startled by her fervor, took a hesitant step back, uncertain.

" Did you feel pain today?" the snow girl asked, her voice soft with sympathy.

"Yes," Jacqueline reluctantly admitted. She didn't fully understand why she was being so honest with this ethereal creature, yet something in her recalled the fairy tales of her childhood, where the magical world did not tolerate lies.

"I set up the nanny, whom I found annoying," she confessed with surprising candor, "and I never expected it to weigh so heavily on me afterward. I don't want to feel this burden anymore. I don't want my soul to ache, even for those who make my life unbearable. I don't want to waste my energy pitying those who aren't worth it. Please, give me the ice," she pleaded, her voice trembling with desperation.

Snowflake took another step back, her delicate form shimmering in the twilight. "I'm sorry, I can't."

"You can't?" Jacqueline echoed, stunned, trying to grasp the meaning of those words. "But you said you brought this ice especially for me, for my heart. For months now, I've wished for nothing more than to feel no regret, no sympathy, no pangs of conscience—just the strength to do what I must to survive. And now, when I finally stand on the brink of that dream, you tell me it's not possible?"

"You don't need this ice," Snowflake replied firmly. "I'm sorry for confusing you, for giving you false hope. When I came here, I didn't fully understand, but now, seeing you, I know—there's no room for ice in your heart. It's still too alive, and your pain cries out louder than anything. Your heart wants to feel and live, but the ice would kill it. It would cut it to pieces and fill it with a deadly cold that will never thaw."

"But I don't want it to thaw!" Jacqueline retorted, her voice laced with anger. "I don't want to remember where I came from or where my brothers are now. What good is a heart that won't let me survive in this place? If I keep it, it will not allow me to be here and I'll be left with nothing but pain, fear, poverty, wandering homeless among those just as destitute and miserable as I am! Do you have any idea what it took for me to get into this house, to earn these people's favor? I'm not willing to lose it all because of some foolish longing that gnaws at my heart. Give me the ice—it's the only way I can stay here."

"But maybe you don't need to stay here," Snowflake suggested gently. "Maybe your place is with your people, among those who share your pain. Together, you can endure the suffering, support one another, and share warmth. Sooner or later, you'll find happiness—together."

"You know," she continued, surprising herself with her own openness, "I live in a magnificent ice palace with the Snow Queen. It's breathtakingly beautiful, the embodiment of perfection. One could live there forever, and yet, more than anything, I want to stay here, in the snow, with my brothers, to survive the winter together with all its joys and spring with all its dangers."

"You can stay wherever you want, but you have no right to decide for me!" Jacqueline shouted, her patience snapping. "I know who I want to be and where I want to go. If you're willing to leave your palace to spend months as a handful of melting snow, then you're nothing but a foolish, spoiled child. You have a treasure, and you don't even appreciate it. I have no way to return to my home, and you're ready to leave yours for a silly dream. If I had what you have, I would do everything imaginable and unimaginable to stay where I belong. You have a huge, beautiful house, and you want to leave it. You are made entirely of ice and snow, and you have begrudged me some small shard of ice!"

"You're right," Snowflake said quietly. "I am made of ice and snow; this is my element, and perhaps I don't deserve anything else. I can't even remember how I came to be in the Snow Queen's castle. I've lived there since early childhood and have long forgotten how to appreciate such a privilege. Maybe you're right—I should stay where I've always been. I'm just a snowflake, and this ice won't harm me, but it will destroy you. You won't find happiness if you lose yourself. I can exist in cold indifference, but you are human; you were made for joy."

With those words, she took a step back. Before Jacqueline could react, Snowflake thrust the shard of ice into her own chest. The pain that erupted within her was like a bolt of lightning, searing through her with the intensity of an electric shock. The air around them exploded into a shower of icy sparks, scattering like shattered glass, and the sky blazed with a sudden stream of northern lights, signaling that the ice fragment had found its mark.

"No!" Jacqueline screamed, her eyes flashing with a predatory gleam. "That ice is mine!"

But as Jacqueline lunged forward, something shifted in Snowflake's gaze. A sharp pang of compassion pierced the icy surface of her fragile heart. The snow sparks around her dimmed, and suddenly, something unbearably hot ignited within her chest, burning like a searing projectile. The force of it knocked her to the ground, leaving her unable to rise. The fire within her raged uncontrollably, consuming her from the inside out, and even the surrounding snow could do nothing to quell the inferno.

"What's happening to you?" Jacqueline cried, rushing to her side and dropping to her knees, her anger forgotten in an instant. Overcome with awe and horror at the sight of another's suffering, she began to scoop up handfuls of snow with her bare hands, frantically pressing them to the little ice girl's torn chest. Nothing else mattered now; someone else's pain eclipsed the entire universe. Jacqueline's thoughts flashed back to the times when her own wounded loved ones had died in her arms, and in this moment, she wanted nothing more than to pour her own lifeblood into another's veins, to fill and revive them.

In a daze, as though observing from a distance, Snowflake watched as a stream of water, melted by the sudden, inexplicable heat, flowed from her chest, washing away the remnants of the ice shards. The Snow Queen's words echoed faintly in her mind: "To answer such requests is only to waste ice." Snowflake had heard tales of how an ice shard, mistakenly placed in a heart that was too kind, would melt, unable to withstand the warmth. Could it be that her own heart was too hot—so hot that it melted the Snow Queen's priceless gift? If so, it would inevitably melt her as well!

As her consciousness began to fade, Snowflake could still hear Jacqueline's frantic pleas.

"Please, little one, don't die," Jacqueline whispered through her tears. "I know what death is, I've seen its horror. Take all the ice in the world, meant for me or anyone else, just don't die. No one should die because of me..."

The stars above shimmered like sparks on the snow, and Snowflake thought that the Queen's magic mirror must have reflected the moment the ice shard had found its target and entered someone's heart. Nothing else mattered now. The Queen had gotten what she wanted and would no longer haunt Jacqueline. The radiance in the sky slowly faded, and the night deepened.

"Am I already dead?" Snowflake wondered faintly. But then, from somewhere far away, she heard Jacqueline's voice.

"Are you alive? See, everything's fine, it's just a thawed patch. Just a small thawed patch."

Snowflake propped herself up on her elbows and glanced down at her chest. A delicate stream of water, like the first drops of a spring thaw, trickled down her icy form, while snowflakes fell gently from the dark sky, as if attempting to mend her wound. She managed a faint smile at Jacqueline, her voice soft and strained.

"Everything's fine," she murmured. And indeed, she felt a sudden lightness within her. The burning pain that had raged in her chest was now replaced by a refreshing coolness, reminiscent of a crisp spring breeze. The snow falling around them seemed to cradle her, lifting her away into the vast, endless realms of some distant, fairy-tale land. Jacqueline hastily wiped away her tears, and as they fell, they mingled with the remnants of ice scattered in the snow.

"You're probably right," Jacqueline admitted with a tentative smile. "I'm not quite ready for an icy heart, and neither are you. So, do you think my place is with my people?"

Snowflake responded quietly. "You know," she began, "I always knew that my kind here, on the mainland, don't live long. And today, I felt it myself. I know that this will happen again when spring comes, and then I won't survive. But today, for the first time, I understood what love is. I felt what it's like to care for someone so deeply that you'd sacrifice everything for them. And I saw how thousands, hundreds of thousands, of other snowflakes descended from the sky to save me. In the ice castle, I never experienced anything like that. I'll stay here so that at the start of each winter, I can be reborn and descend from the sky to those who need me. Is that so little?"

Jacqueline shrugged, uncertainty clouding her expression. "Do you think they'll accept me after I've been here?" she asked, her voice tinged with doubt.

"Someone will," Snowflake replied with quiet confidence. "And more importantly, you'll discover that you can be among your own people without needing an icy heart. Is that so little?"

"You're right," Jacqueline whispered. "I miss home terribly. More than anything, I want to go back."

She scooped up a handful of snow, letting it rest in her palm. The snowflakes sparkled playfully, casting glimmers of light on her face, then began to melt, weeping softly between her fingers. The drops fell into the snowdrifts, and the snow, as if in response, quickly closed the tiny wounds with new, intricately carved snowflakes. The snow continued its gentle healing, turning bleeding streams into healing ones, and washing away the remnants of ice. The flakes falling from the sky grew larger, their descent weaving the sky and earth together in a single, swirling dance of winter, like the familiar, comforting blanket of a childhood dream.

A Tale of a Forgotten Memory

"But have you made your final decision?" Danka asked him, perhaps for the tenth time. Her eyes, filled with both anxiety and sorrow, pierced Goran, filling him once more with a deep sense of guilt. Again, he tried to convince her and himself that his decision was the only correct one, the best one possible, and entirely safe.

"We have already agreed on everything," he repeated, his voice insistent.

"But you don't know her at all!" Danka exclaimed. "Perhaps she harbors ill intentions? What if she's a witch, exploiting your weakness to destroy you?"

"You too?" Goran's eyes flashed, revealing something sinister and frightening, lurking deep within him. Danka involuntarily shuddered. "Do you also think that forest fairies are witches?"

"No, not at all," she quickly reassured him. "That's not what I meant. I fear she might be a witch in the guise of a fairy. We don't even know for sure if she is who she claims she is."

"I can recognize a true fairy," Goran said coldly. "Don't forget what kind of blood runs in my veins."

His words sounded like a challenge, and Danka knew well the reason for this. Goran was the son of a vila, a forest fairy taken treacherously as a wife by his human father. From ancient beliefs, Danka knew vilas typically did not harm humans and could even aid them. Yet, rumors also spoke of how overly fond these forest beings could become of men, and how jealous they could be of their earthly lovers.

"Even if she is a real vila and wishes to help you," Danka began timidly, "don't you think she could erase all your memories, making you forget about me and about our home, so that you never return?"

"I am the son of a vila," Goran repeated stubbornly. "No fairy will ever harm me."

"I'm not talking about harm," Danka explained patiently. She finally looked up from her work—carefully straining the curd mass to separate it from the whey. Danka made the best cheese in the village—fragrant, melting in the mouth better than any sweets, intoxicating with its spicy aroma. She set the future cheese aside, wiped her hands on her apron, and sat down at the table opposite him.

"A vila might believe she's doing you a favor," Danka continued insistently. "What if she decides your place is with them and not here? She might think you'd be happier if you forgot us all. But do you want to forget this life—forget me—and know I will remain here alone?"

Her anxiety wafted to him like a light draft, disturbing the comfort of their village home, spreading fear like a harmful infection. Goran couldn't deny that Danka's fears had merit. Legends of the vilas' kindness coexisted with tales of their cunning, and no one fully understood how their magic could affect a person—even one not entirely ordinary.

"She won't be able to take me with her," Goran asserted, striving to sound confident. "A man cannot be a vila; he cannot fly. Thus, I could never reach where the fairies dwell. Only serpents can ascend there, and I am clearly not a serpent. Besides, the vila promised me that we're only talking about my first five years. Those five years brought nothing but nightmares into my life, and I don't want to—and can't—remember them!" he said angrily, turning away.

"I know, my dear, I know," Danka responded, helplessly bowing her head before his grief. In such moments, she felt her powerlessness acutely, as one does in the face of an incurable disease—a wall separating the patient from those who love him infinitely. Danka knew precisely what her young husband wanted to forget, and the deep wound in his heart that he carried throughout his life, unable to rid himself of it.

His mother was indeed a vila—a winged forest sorceress who, like her other tribesmen, lived high in the mountains, inaccessible to people. Yet, like many of her kind, she sometimes ventured into human realms, where she met her future husband, Svetozar, Goran's father. Madly in love with the golden-haired fairy beauty, Svetozar took her wings, turning her into an almost ordinary woman. Only her horse hooves, carefully hidden under long white garments, betrayed her forest origins.

Svetozar made her his wife, and soon, little Goran was born. However, as is often the case with vilas, the former fairy began to grow weary of human life. She longed for the endless forest expanses, the mountain peaks piercing the sky, the thundering walls of waterfalls, and the uneven squares of fields bordered by forests and dotted with villages. Svetozar, already a reveler and a drunkard, grew more reckless, seeing the indifference of his young wife. During one of his sprees, he boasted to his fellow villagers that he was married to a real vila.

The village men took his boast with skepticism, but a severe drought soon struck, followed by famine. Desperately searching for a scapegoat, the villagers recalled Svetozar's story and descended on his home, demanding he surrender his "witch" wife. In vain, the now-sober Svetozar insisted he was joking and married to an ordinary woman. The crowd stormed his house, determined to test his words, and cornered the vila. She rushed away from the people and managed to slip past them but snagged the hem of her long white dress on a nail, revealing her slender horse's hoof.

"Witch!" the crowd roared. "She will destroy our village!"

In a senseless, bestial rage, the men attacked the foreigner with pitchforks and axes. They blocked her path to the gate, and the vila, driven into a corner, rushed into the barn and locked the door from the inside.

"Come out, damned evil spirit!" the crowd roared. "You will pay for our suffering!"

Svetozar's shouts fell on deaf ears. Realizing his danger, he retreated, knowing the enraged crowd would tear him apart if he persisted. Meanwhile, one of the angry men hurled a fiery torch into the barn. Flames glided along the plank door, gratefully picking up the handout, grabbed it with greedy tongues, crawled towards the eaves, and flared up. This scene burned itself into little Goran's memory. The five-year-old boy watched, frozen in horror, as black shadows spread, breaking out beams and corroding woody flesh.

Recovering from his stupor, Svetozar belatedly rushed back into the house and threw the wings he had taken from the vila into the burning barn. Gasping, the fairy grabbed them and tried to take flight, but the collapsing barn roof buried her beneath a heap of burning boards...

After the death of the vila, the villagers remained relentless, constantly taunting Svetozar with the claim that he was raising the "son of a witch." Cowardly and weak-willed, fearing more for himself than for the child, Svetozar sent little Goran to a distant village where his mother lived, a place where no one knew about his origins. From that moment, Goran heard nothing about his father and, frankly, did not want to. He held his father responsible for his mother's death and, even after his grandmother's passing, never tried to find him. He lived in the village, indistinguishable from the other villagers, growing up, establishing a household, mastering the craft of pottery, and eventually falling in love with the beautiful Danka, whose golden hair somehow reminded him of his deceased mother.

Goran did not immediately reveal the secret of his origin to his beloved. When he finally did, Danka was neither horrified nor proud of his magical roots. She did not curiously ask if he had any miraculous powers but instead reacted to his grief with deep, feminine sympathy. She couldn't imagine exactly what he had felt that year, but she knew that even many years later, the nightmare he had experienced returned to Goran as vividly as if it had happened yesterday. The past, surging from oblivion, filled the present with poison, draining its vitality and absorbing it, coming to life before their eyes. In those moments, it seemed to Danka that some unknown witchcraft was tearing Goran from the happy simplicity of their daily life and casting him into an abyss of horror.

For the first time, a way out of this abyss appeared—a light force capable of overcoming the dark magic of memory. One day, while gathering brushwood in the forest, Goran met a vila—a fabulously beautiful woman with hair that cascaded to the ground. She seemed the very embodiment of the forest, infused with its scents, breathing with the primordial power of burgeoning life, and blossoming with the beauty and fragrance of all the flowers in the world. Everything about her was perfect, unearthly, and yet familiar—the inexpressible voice of blood, the call that Goran felt more keenly than ever before.

Learning of his grief, the vila offered her help—a miracle Goran had never dared to dream of. She promised to grant him a new memory of the first five years of his life, years that had forever poisoned his soul with endless nightmares.

"You won't forget anything that happened to you after those years. You will remember the life you have lived up to this day. You will even remember that you agreed to change your memory. Only one piece of it will disappear—the part that doesn't allow you to be happy," the vila said, her voice like a forest stream, gurgling in his ears and filling his soul with a newfound hope. Even if her words were not entirely true, even if the cost to rid himself of this curse was high, Goran felt he could no longer abandon this hope.

He caught Danka's anxious gaze once more and lowered his eyes. Tomorrow, tomorrow he would go into the forest to pursue his dream!

"If I forget these five years, I will lose nothing," he spoke again, turning to Danka, unsure if he was trying to convince her or himself. "I cut them out of my life a long time ago.

None of the people who knew me then will come here, and I will never return to them. I have lived without them as if they never existed, and only the memory—this damned memory—is the one thing I still can't escape. You know how long I have dreamed of forgetting all this!"

Danka nodded, trying to soothe her anxiety. Perhaps he was right? The vision of a happy life, unmarred by terrible memories, appeared before her with startling clarity. Maybe a miracle would indeed happen, and the innocent serenity that reigned in their village would finally enter her husband's heart, filling him with joy and peace.

"Yes, you're right, you should try it," she said, attempting an encouraging smile.

* * *

Dawn was stealthily seeping through the shutters, and Goran knew that as soon as he opened the window, it would pour into the room with streams of light, lush greenery sparkling in its rays and invigorating morning freshness. Slipping quietly out of the house, he climbed the hill and took a long look at his village, as if afraid he might be saying goodbye to it forever. He did not want to wake Danka, realizing that try as she might, she would not be able to hide her fear and anxiety. Deep down, he feared his wife might be right.

Goran gazed at the inviting road playfully winding through the lowland, at the dark red, sometimes blackened, tiled roofs of impeccably white houses, standing out brightly against the green backdrop. He admired the wooded slope of the mountain, at the foot of which white square houses also huddled. From afar, it seemed that at any moment they could be overwhelmed by the green waves of the forest pouring from the top. Goran turned his gaze to the other side—to the smooth grass of the hillock, where, no longer covered by trees, the stone foundations and basements of houses looked like fortress walls, and the huts themselves seemed too light against the backdrop of their massive, uneven masonry.

He admired the chapel, which seemed very tiny from here, the paths winding through the hills, the wooden decks embedded into the gentle slope, and the railings of the stairs leading along the hill to the village church. Everything here exuded an indescribable feeling of comfort, safety, and peace. Familiar, deeply familiar, yet always surprising him with its quiet beauty, this place had become for Goran the embodiment of life itself, its main and only support. And Danka, the person dearest and closest to him, was waiting for him there.

"I'm not doing this just for myself, I'm doing it for both of us," he whispered resolutely and headed toward the forest.

At the very outskirts of the village, he saw boys making a small bonfire, and the sight of flame slashed through his heart with a revived memory. A bright image, indistinguishable from reality, flashed before him again with stunning clarity. Here is a raging flame that tears up the air, melting it and making it tremble as if in horror. Objects and faces were distorted in this trembling, but even through its blurry ripples, he saw the figure of his mother engulfed in flames. The figure of his father was forever imprinted in his memory—confused, face white with horror, hastily throwing a pair of wings into the fire.

Goran watched as the golden-haired fairy, like a living tongue of flame, darted out of the inferno, trailed by a shower of hot sparks. It seemed that just a little more and she would rise above these insignificant mortals, ascending to the light, to freedom, to her native element. But at that moment, a deafening crash resounded, as if the very planet were bursting from within, and something vast and indistinguishable—like a colossal piece of fire—plummeted from above, colliding with her ethereal form. The fiery whirlwind, ravenous at the sight of a new prey, roared and surged downward, consuming everything in its path.

Goran heard himself scream—a heart-rending cry of "Mom!" He remembered his father's hands seizing his shoulders as tightly as if they were steel claws. Then there was only darkness, sundered by flames, and it seemed that in the entire world, there was nothing but this consuming darkness...

Goran shook his head, trying to banish the haunting memories. The forest around him whispered with a gentle rustle, filled to the core with the morning sun, which had not yet wiped the dew from the grass.

"This is the last time," he vowed to himself. "The last time I revisit this."

He went deeper into the forest, which seemed to part in gracious obedience, its leaves sparkling with silver flecks, casting playful shadows that beckoned into the verdant depths. As he advanced, it was as though he was becoming part of this enchanted realm, yearning to merge with its mysterious essence. Suddenly, the trees began to whisper and sway, and birds, startled by the sudden movement, erupted from their perches in a flurry of wings and song, as though welcoming a forest fairy. From the depths of the woods, she emerged into a clearing, more resplendent than ever, a true mistress of the forest. Her hair cascaded like a shimmering waterfall, and her smile seemed to capture the very brilliance of the sun.

"Hello, Goran," she greeted him with such warmth that his anxieties melted away at the sound of her voice. "Are you truly prepared to fulfill your promise?"

"Prepared!" he affirmed with conviction. "Take it, and take it forever!"

The vila's smile grew radiant once more. She approached Goran, resting her hands on his shoulders, and with a fervent kiss on his forehead—like a mother's kiss to her only child—he felt a jolt of pain, sharp and sudden, piercing through his head and sinking into his heart. Sensing his distress, the vila enfolded him in her embrace. Her garments carried the cool scent of mountain streams, and her hair was redolent with wildflowers. For a fleeting moment, Goran felt as though he had drifted into a tranquil slumber. But as reality's sounds and colors began to seep back in, the vila gently withdrew, taking a step back.

"What do you remember?" she asked softly.

Goran tensed as a flood of memories surged before him—conversations with Danka, her worried gaze, his quiet departure in the early morning, a final glance at his pottery wheel. And there he was, standing at the forest's edge, gazing at his beloved village. If this was indeed his memory, he recalled it all.

"What do you remember from your childhood?" the vila inquired, as if reading his thoughts.

The question pierced deep into his consciousness, racing through years in a heartbeat. Suddenly, a fresh, intoxicating breeze of recollection enveloped him. He saw the earth stretched out beneath him, an awe-inspiring canvas of beauty—majestic and minuscule all at once. The mountains rose like sculpted mounds, shrouded in green waves of forest where individual trees were barely discernible. Their bases cut like a wavy ribbon into the frozen surface of the lakes—crystal smooth, a blend of blue and green that mirrored the earth and sky.

White patches of bare rock appeared on the mountains, crowned by fortresses, as if growing out of water and stone, that seemed like toys. The rivers, like the veins of the planet swollen with water, carved their way through the landscape, racing from the mountains to the plains. There, they meandered lazily, their courses expanding into gentle, reflective pools that skirted tiny human settlements.

Goran remembered the sensation of flight and its unparalleled thrill. The wind lifted him, hurling him into the boundless sky, into the boundless heights, the limits of which were impossible to reach. The wind raged, whistled in his ears, threw scalding cold jets of air into his face, as he soared higher, surpassing eagles, until he began his descent, bathed in sunlight. The earth slowly came into focus—the trees, fields, and village houses became clearer, and nature's breath grew more palpable, embracing him with maternal warmth.

He marveled at the stone churches, ancient rock paintings, and monasteries embedded in the stone. He enjoyed watching the lakes grow, shifting from blue-green ribbons to shimmering ripples that reflected the earth's beauty.

Despite everything, Goran could not doubt the truth of what he experienced—it was undeniably his own memory. Each scene was etched into his being, resonating with every fiber of his soul. He recalled the exhilaration of diving steeply toward the bridge, which from above had appeared as fragile as a thread stretched between two matchsticks. He remembered the glimmering stones beneath the crystal-clear mountain lake, the mingling streams of cold wind and warm sunlight, interwoven into a continuous thread of childish wonder.

"Did you give me your memory?" he asked, his gaze fixed in astonishment on the vila.

"Don't worry, my memory remains with me," she replied with a gentle smile. "This is the memory of the dead vila; she no longer has need of it. I thought it might bring you a touch of happiness."

"How can I ever thank you?" Goran breathed out, still in awe.

"No thanks are necessary," the vila smiled once more. "I do not seek human gratitude. I saw your suffering and was glad to offer my aid."

"You are truly a sorceress!" Goran exclaimed, still not believing his ears. "If you ever need any help, know that you can always count on me."

With these words, he turned to head back. The forest, once merely friendly, now felt profoundly familiar, as though it had revealed its deepest essence to him. Goran felt himself merge with its very being, the profound happiness that enveloped him at that moment seemed boundless. He returned to his village, his heart brimming with love and joy, eager to share it unreservedly with those he cherished.

Danka rushed to meet him, her arms flinging around his neck.

"Do you remember me?" she asked with hopeful eyes, searching his face.

"I remember, my dear, of course I remember," Goran soothed her. "I have never forgotten you."

A sigh of relief, light as a breeze, escaped her, giving way to joy—boundless as sunlight streaming from the heavens.

* * *

Time drifted forward at its own steady, unhurried pace. The sun yielded to rain, and the once vibrant green leaves matured into a tapestry of rich, autumnal hues. The clay on the potter's wheel spun, leaving the familiar, dirty streaks on Goran's hands—brown stains that served as a constant reminder of his own mortal nature: clay, earth, dust, and decay. Similar stains, though white, adorned Danka's hands as she strained boiled milk in preparation for cheese. The soft, yielding curd, drying marks on the hands, the sunlight filtering through the shutters, and the gentle warmth that blanketed the earth after rain—all these elements wove together to form the fabric of Goran's daily existence, simple and predictable in its every detail.

Yet, the more routine and predictable his life became, the more vividly Goran found himself recalling the images of his childhood. He knew well that these were not truly his childhood memories, yet he had no other recollections from that time. The sensation of flight, deeply ingrained in his being along with these memories, resonated through every cell, filling his veins with a yearning that threatened to burst forth, not as streams of blood, but as torrents of air, longing for freedom and space. The currents of air felt confined within his human form, yearning to merge with the boundless blue, to lose themselves in the winds, and to dissolve into the infinite elements.

"You are not a vila," Goran reminded himself. "You have never been one and cannot become one. You cannot fly."

But another, treacherous thought soon took root in his mind. Though he was undeniably human and could not become a vila, he was the son of a forest fairy. Perhaps, he mused, he might possess serpentine abilities. Could he be a serpent in human guise, destined to soar through the skies, summon rain during droughts, and protect the crops? The more these thoughts overwhelmed him, the more insipid his current life seemed.

The village, always so familiar, began to feel increasingly like a prison. The wooden decks on the hills, once symbols of comfort, now appeared as manacles chaining the ground. The village's openness to the wind felt illusory as if the very space was constricted, hemmed in by walls and narrow streets.

More and more often, Goran found himself yearning to escape the maze of roads and fences, to embrace the true expanse of the open space. He longed to feel his breath meld with the breath of the earth, to be called by the forests, and to be cradled by the sky, carried like a cloud over the mountains and lakes. He ventured more frequently into the forest, hoping to encounter the vila once more, to discover whether he might truly possess the abilities of a serpent. This hope, a powerful force enveloping his entire being, grew insistent; without it, he felt he could not find happiness.

He loved Danka—or at least he believed he did. Yet she was as much a part of the village as the soft curd mass she worked with. Goran fantasized about transforming into a full-fledged serpent, lifting her above the ground, and showing her the world from above the ground. He envisioned sharing his domain with her, revealing the forests and mountains from above, tracing the rivers' threads across the green expanse, and letting her see the snowy peaks glittering in the sun. He would lead her, like a queen, into their mountainous realm, where instead of mirrors she would look at the wall of a waterfall, and he would guide her to the very source of the streams cascading into the abyss. Only then would she truly understand him. Her loving, responsive heart would embrace the magical world of nature, and their love would become boundless.

This was Goran's dream as he wandered through the forest, while Danka waited for him in their small village home.

Flowers bloomed in the garden, chickens clucked nearby, and occasionally a goat bleated in the pen—the same goat whose milk Danka used to craft the finest cheese in the village. She sensed Goran drifting away from her, powerless to bridge the growing distance. Despite her efforts to create comfort in their home and her patient vigils on the porch, her fears were realized. As the sun dipped below the horizon and twilight thickened in the lowlands, Goran was still absent.

Suddenly, Danka heard footsteps—unfamiliar and close. A young man, barely more than a boy, approached her porch.

"Excuse me, does the potter Goran live here?" he asked loudly.

"Here," Danka replied, a hint of surprise in her voice. She had never seen this young man in their village before and wondered how he knew Goran and what he wanted from her husband.

"I have come a long way searching for him," the stranger said. "My name is Radovan, or Rado. I am Goran's half-brother; we share the same father."

"You shouldn't have come here," Danka responded, a touch of fear in her voice. "Much has changed recently, and my husband no longer remembers you."

"He doesn't need to remember me," Rado tried to explain. "He never knew me. After his father sent him to this village, he married an earthly woman—my mother. I was born from that union. Before he died, my father told me for the first time that I had an older brother, the son of a forest fairy. I know how his mother died, and I can't tell you how much it pains me. I must tell Goran how repentant his father was before his death for the grief he caused them both."

"There's no need for that," Danka interrupted. "My husband spent years trying to forget the nightmare he experienced. Finally, he found a way to rid himself of that part of his memory. Forgive me, but he will no longer remember your father or the death of his mother. I beg you, under no circumstances, remind him of this."

Rado listened, somewhat surprised, but did not argue.

"Okay," he nodded solemnly. "I give my word that I will never remind my brother of what he worked so hard to forget. But let me at least see him, even from afar. He is my only brother, my blood and flesh. Perhaps, getting to know each other, we can become friends, but I no longer hope for more."

Danka hesitated for a moment. Maybe if Goran made a new friend, he would become more attached to the village and stop his constant wandering through the forests. Maybe Rado could help her find him?

"He's gone," Danka said, barely holding back tears. "Since the vila gave him another memory, Goran has been venturing into the forests more and more often. I don't know when he will return."

Rado read the despair in her voice and said decisively, "Don't be afraid, I will find him. I will definitely find him. While I enjoyed my mother's warmth and father's care, my brother grew up alone in a foreign land. I must make up for what he has been deprived of all these years."

Danka smiled gratefully in response.

* * *

Rado plunged deeper into the forest, pushing through the dense thicket. The further he went, the more motionless the trees seemed. The forest seemed frozen in an ominous silence, afraid to stir. Not a single breeze rustled the leaves, and even the air felt glassy in anxious anticipation. Undeterred, Rado pressed on, the undergrowth growing denser and darker. Night descended swiftly, enveloping everything in its shadow.

Suddenly, amidst the darkness, Rado glimpsed a flicker of flame. One, then another—flames sprouted before him like wildfire. As if repelled by the fire, the forest retreated, dissolving into thin air, revealing village houses in its place. The flickering firelight illuminated the contours of a wooden fence, a low hut, and courtyard buildings. One of the structures burned fiercely, and Rado heard a heart-rending scream emanating from the heart of the blaze. Instinctively, he wanted to rush to help, but a crowd stood between him and the fire like an impenetrable wall.

Rado turned helplessly, his eyes widening as he saw his own father staring back at him with a vacant gaze. It was unmistakably him, though younger, with an expression of horror as he watched the unfolding events. Recovering from his stupor, the father seized a pair of enormous wings from somewhere and hurled them into the flames.

Miraculously, a female figure shot up like an arrow from the inferno, casting off burning embers as she soared toward the sky, blackening in the distance. But the fire, like a vengeful beast, surged after her and struck her chest. Her fragile body convulsed, then froze in midair before slowly, too slowly, plummeting back into the fiery abyss.

The flames consumed everything, their tongues sprouting from the ground like fiery flowers. Acrid smoke filled the air, and it was impossible to find an escape from it. Rado suddenly realized the crowd had vanished, leaving nothing but darkness and flames. The fire encircled him, entangled him in a ring as if wanting to incinerate the entire universe. In desperation, Rado dashed through the fiery tongues, searching for a way out. He spotted a gap between two pillars of fire and lunged for it, feeling as though he had narrowly escaped death itself, miraculously slipping between its millstones.

He ran until exhaustion forced him to the ground, where he saw the uneven paving stones of a street beneath him. Rising in surprise, the young man found himself in a city. The dim light from street lamps cast a feeble glow on the stone walls of the houses. The city was ghostly empty, as if all life had been erased from it by someone's unseen hand. There was no fire here, but the air remained musty and stale, the night's coolness unable to break through the suffocating atmosphere.

Rado walked slowly forward, straining to catch the source of a noise that seemed very close. He turned around but saw nothing. Suddenly, something rustled past like a gust of wind, brushing against his legs before darting forward into the ominously empty street. Rado instinctively pressed himself against the wall and only then noticed: a horde of rats scurrying along the paving stones. He watched their backs with wide eyes, then slowly followed. The rats turned into an alley, and Rado cautiously peered into it, trying to discern what had attracted them. Near a black wall, untouched by the lantern's light, mutilated human bodies were piled. The rats busily swarmed over them, their tails flickering in the faint reflections of the street lamps.

Only now did Rado realize a plague was ravaging the city. The stench of decay hung in the air, and that was why the streets were so eerily empty. Death incarnate reigned here, with no one left to remove the corpses from the streets. From the pile of dead bodies, groans of those mistakenly cast there while still alive began to rise. In horror, Rado dashed away through the cobbled streets of the dead city, but the labyrinth of narrow streets seemed endless. There was no village or forest, only the endless maze of stone and shadows.

Desperate and nearly mad with fear, Rado struck the stone wall with all his might, frantically hoping to break through the nightmare surrounding him. To his surprise, the wall gave way, swaying before it collapsed. Rado lunged forward, as one leaps into an abyss—desperately and irrevocably. Another moment, and he found himself back in the forest, now at night, with only weak starlight filtering through the trees. In this faint light, Rado saw an incomparably beautiful woman in white robes, her haughty smile chilling.

"Are you a vila?" Rado exhaled, his voice trembling.

"Yes, I am the keeper of these places," came her reply. "What are you doing in my forest at this hour?"

"I'm looking for my brother, Goran," Rado answered more firmly.

"Goran has no brothers among men," the vila responded coldly.

"I am the son of his father; the same blood flows in me as in him!" Rado retorted, stepping closer. "You shouldn't lure people into your domain. It would be better if you figured out what's happening in your forest. I saw burning villages and cities plagued by disease."

"You'll see more than just that," the vila laughed sinisterly. "For many years, I've been collecting terrible memories of suffering people. They were willing to give half their lives to forget these memories, and I gave them that relief. I carefully gathered all the hell that tormented them. And finally, the last to come to me was my own nephew, the son of my poor sister, who died before his eyes at the hands of madmen..."

The vila paused, her voice dropping to a whisper.

"Even then, I vowed to avenge her death and ensure that everyone would experience the nightmare my sister endured. Now my dream is coming true. I have collected enough horrors to blanket the entire earth. They will spread from this forest, and what tormented a few will become the burden of all."

Rado listened in horror, his suspicions now confirmed by the vila's chilling confession. The hell he had found himself in while searching for Goran was not reality but a memory— a revived memory of his brother and others who had sought to forget their pasts. Now, this memory was creeping through the forest like a black cloud, inching closer to people's homes.

"Stop this!" Rado shouted at the vila. "You took away the suffering of some innocent people only to make others, just as innocent, suffer! Think about it—little children, young girls, and helpless old people will be trapped in this nightmare. You bring pain and destruction to all living things. Stop before it's too late!"

"Too late!" the vila responded menacingly. "It's too late now. I've waited too long for this, and there's nothing you can do to stop it." With these words, she vanished into the darkness.

The nightmare enveloped Rado once more, materializing from nowhere and saturating the entire space. Again, he saw the burning barn and heard the women's screams. Was this how his half-brother's mother had perished?

"It's an illusion, just a memory," he told himself, turning away. "It happened many years ago, and I can't change anything."

However, the smell of burning was so strong, so pungent and acrid, that it was impossible to doubt its reality. Rado saw two wings thrown into the flames of the burning building. He knew what would happen next. A wave of pain and compassion swept over him, and, pushing through the crowd, Rado rushed to the barn. He no longer cared how real this vision was. This had become his reality, a nightmare from which he could not escape, and Rado wanted only one thing—to save the unfortunate, innocent fairy trapped in the burning building.

He shoved aside the frenzied people and, feeling the scorching breath of fire on his face, began to unfurl the burning beams and hurl them aside, dodging the voracious flames. A little more, just a little more—and he would accomplish what his father could not—he would save the fairy. With surprise, Rado noticed how the firebrands he cast aside evaporated into the air without burning him at all.

"Hold on!" he shouted, breaking through the fiery wall with increasing boldness. But with every step he took, the world around him changed. The fire began to melt, dissolve, and disappear, retreating before the encroaching night forest.

Rado looked around. No, he had not saved the beautiful fairy, and she was not there.

"Fool!" he heard the voice of the other vila, the deceased's sister, from somewhere above. "You cannot change the past. It has already happened. This is just a memory."

"Yes, but I can change this damn memory!" Rado shouted into the void. Once again, he found himself in the plague-stricken city, and now, unafraid, he dashed through the labyrinthine streets, searching for the alley with the dead-end wall. He knew there were still living people among the corpses who needed his help. The streets were so narrow that Rado could touch both walls with his hands. Rats darted underfoot, brushing against him with their nimble tails, but he paid them no heed. He reached the pile of bodies and, closing his eyes, plunged his hands into the plague-ridden mass. Another moment—and instead of cobblestones, his fingers felt the damp forest soil...

The darkness finally cleared, and Rado stood in a moonlit clearing. Opposite him, slightly confused, stood the vila.

"I'm deeply pained by what happened to your sister," Rado said quietly. "I know that humans will forever be guilty before you, and no power can heal such a wound. This memory cannot be erased without a trace. It is inescapable, and yet, as you see, it is not omnipotent."

"You rushed to save my sister, not even knowing whether it was possible or what would happen next?" the vila asked, barely concealing her surprise. "Why would you, a human, do that?"

"That's why I couldn't just watch another living being suffer," Rado replied. "People are different. My brother Goran has a wonderful, loving wife, and she is human. Yet Goran loves her, and human blood flows also in his veins. I know that vilas don't usually harm people, and I believe you don't want to make innocent people suffer either."

The fairy looked at him thoughtfully and, without a word, spread her beautiful wings and soared into the sky. The black fog had almost entirely dissipated, with only a few tattered remnants drifting between the trees, as if seeking their real owners. These tatters, pitiful and no longer threatening, obediently floated into his palms on the breeze...

Goran turned around, feeling a slight movement in the wind behind him. A wisp of black fog emerged from the thicket and enveloped him momentarily. A sharp pain pierced his temples, radiating into his heart, and suddenly, Goran remembered the tongues of fire and the faces of people contorted with rage. The memory pricked him slightly, but the images now seemed distant, receding into the past. They no longer had the power to dominate the present and only stirred a quiet melancholy of loneliness in his heart.

For a moment, Goran felt like a little boy in need of consolation, and immediately, the image of Danka, so tender and loving, filled his mind. Danka! How worried she must have been about him! How long had he wandered in the forest, leaving her all alone in the village? Stricken by this thought, Goran hurried back. Soon he emerged onto the road leading to the village, when he suddenly saw the figure of a young man approaching. Something familiar in his features made Goran pause, then quicken his pace towards the stranger. The young man noticed and smiled broadly, also hurrying towards him.

A Tale of the Rag Doll

THE LAST RAY OF LIGHT CREPT TIMIDLY across the floor before vanishing into the closing door. Oppressive darkness settled heavily in the utility room. Elina shivered and curled herself into a ball deep within the box, hiding among the props, as only she could. Her absolute plasticity allowed her to vanish into folds and crevices where others could not follow—a unique talent, yet it came at a price. Unlike the others in the puppet theater, Elina had no wire frame to give her form, no wooden arms and legs—albeit awkward and angular, making every movement unnaturally constrained, but giving a sense of weight, support, and strength.

Some dolls, as formless as Elina in appearance, at least possessed hearts—small, sturdy centers of tin or plastic, placed with care inside their chests for balance. But when Elina was crafted, her maker had seemingly forgotten that essential gift. If she had a heart at all, it was no different than the rest of her: soft, pliable, and vulnerable, offering no resistance to even the gentlest blow. Vulnerability was her constant companion from the moment of her creation. She was open, defenseless, unable to shield herself from cruelty, from dangers—real or imagined—that lurked in every shadow. Time and again, life had reinforced this feeling.

Yet it was precisely this softness that made Elina's talent unique. Unlike the others, she could feel every nuance of her master's hand with an uncanny sensitivity. The other dolls, rigid and unyielding, performed their roles as they were moved, but Elina became her master's gestures. With every cell, even the tiniest piece of fabric and every thread of her pliable body, she felt the smallest movement of his fingers, and absorbed every intention, even before it fully formed, an intonation that had not yet sounded in his voice.

Elina got used to the role, as one gets used to a new body. It was as if she no longer acted, but lived, inhabited by a consciousness not her own. This consciousness grew and thrived, fed by the master's presence—by his hand, so strong and independent, providing the stability she so desperately craved. With that hand guiding her, Elina felt invincible. In those moments, the horizon opened up before her with the boundless perfection of talent. She came to life, blossomed, spiritualizing any character with her acting, infusing it with life so real that it felt as though it was more real than herself.

Yet, as always, the performance would end. The puppeteer's hand would withdraw, and with it, her sense of safety. The world that had seemed boundless just moments before turned cold and hostile, filled once more with the threat of betrayal, disappointment, and abandonment. These fears weren't mere illusions—they were the brutal truths of her existence. She had known betrayal all too well. Time and again, promises made to her were broken. Leading roles she had been assured of slipped away, and she was left discarded, forgotten at the bottom of the chest like some useless, discarded trinket.

The other dolls also faced their share of neglect, but they were stronger and more resilient. Inside them, they felt the firm pulse of their springy wire frames or the reassuring weight of their solid hearts. They laughed off misfortune, knowing that no hardship could truly harm them. Their moods might shift with a setback, but their structure remained intact. A puppeteer's hand could bend them, but not fold them in half, turn them into a shapeless doormat-like lump, and certainly it could not break them. They seemed invulnerable to any trials and went through life effortlessly—something that Elina could never do.

Of course, their "thick skin" could not help but affect their performance. Their movements on stage seemed unnatural and angular, sometimes too sharp and sweeping, and sometimes, on the contrary, frozen in stupid immobility. Their joints clacked and knocked as they moved, and sometimes, it seemed as though they resented the hand that controlled them, eager to break free and dance a clumsy, graceless dance of their own—a dance of liberation, void of elegance but filled with defiant joy.

Elina had never craved the wild, reckless freedom that others seemed to yearn for. What she longed for was protection— a steady hand to guide her, a presence she could lean on with gratitude. All she wanted was to bring her master's vision to life with the grace and perfection that only she possessed. Yet, over time, she found herself pulled from the chest less and less often. Unlike the other dolls, who unceremoniously thrust themselves into the puppeteer's grasp, Elina remained silent and still, forgotten beneath a mound of props. Left abandoned, she retreated inward, sinking deeply into her own suffering.

The sense of injustice that consumed her was overwhelming. Elina was certain that this was not just her personal torment but the very foundation of the universe. The world itself was built on injustice, thrusting its cruelty upon her like an unchangeable truth. And strangely, in this abyss of hopelessness, she discovered a bittersweet comfort. She reveled in her misery, embracing it with a kind of grim satisfaction, as if she were performing for some invisible audience, showcasing the depth of her sorrow.

Grievance, she believed, was the only constant in life, and this belief grew stronger with each passing day. People and dolls alike were treacherous, indifferent, and selfish—rare exceptions existed, but their rarity only confirmed the rule. Even those who once valued and helped her would inevitably fall victim to the world's flaws. They would break under its weight or, worse, become just like everyone else, and their inept help would only prolong her suffering.

Expecting nothing from life, trusting no one, Elina curled herself into a nearly perfect ball, once again feeling the plasticity that defined her—and with it, her vulnerability. Here, in the dark chest, she could at least shield herself from the cruelty of the world. She could retreat into her private, somber refuge, where suffering was certain, but at least familiar and, in a way, safe.

Suddenly, a creak pierced the silence, followed by a sharp beam of light that struck her eyes. The chest door swung open, and through the jumble of the shapeless rags of the props, Elina glimpsed the familiar hand of the puppeteer. She barely restrained herself from leaping forward and clutching that hand, pressing her whole body against the saving support.

"Come now, my dear, you've been lying here far too long," the puppeteer said gently, lifting her from the rags. "We have an exclusive performance for the children of a wealthy lord, and I know no one can do it better than you."

Elina trembled, not daring to believe her ears. Her moment had come—an opportunity to perform before special, distinguished guests. This could be the beginning of a new life, one she had never allowed herself to dream of until now. If she succeeded, if the young audience adored her, perhaps she would finally claim the leading role in the troupe forever. She would perform in every production, breathing life into new characters, giving form to others' ideas with her unmatched talent. At times, Elina even dared to imagine that the roles she played might one day give something back to her—imbue her with the strength and confidence to move freely, no longer needing the puppeteer's hand for every step.

But for now, she sat gratefully on his palm, her legs dangling as he carried her out of the chest and into the wide, bright world beyond. Hope, that fragile and treacherous thing she had vowed countless times never to embrace again, ignited once more in her heart. Against her better judgment, her imagination began spinning images of success, recognition, and—most intoxicating of all—acceptance and love. The very thing she craved most, love, shimmered before her like a distant star. And Elina's delicate soul trembling in anticipation of her cherished audience—someone who would finally see her, appreciate her, and offer her at least a little gratitude.

Out of habit, she steeled herself, forbidding hope to take root, but the moment her guard slipped, thoughts rushed in, one after another, and her emotions obediently embraced the anticipation of happiness. For Elina, happiness was hidden even in the rehearsal—a clumsy, unfinished echo of future success. It seemed inconceivable that something good could happen to her, though she had often seen it bestowed upon others. Yet in her life, in her fate, the idea of complete happiness felt almost absurd. Still, she poured all her energy into this last hope, this final chance to change her destiny.

At last, the day of the premiere arrived. Elina played the role of Cinderella, and the part came to her so naturally, so organically, that she didn't feel as though she were acting at all. Was it really acting when she conveyed the quiet yearning, the deeply suffered secret expectation of long-overdue reward for hard work? Hadn't she, like Cinderella, toiled endlessly, driven by the desperate hope for recognition? And now, would she finally receive what she deserved?

The fairy tale unfolded around her in all its royal splendor. The ball glittered, and the prince—though not a real one, merely another actor like her—stared at her with glassy, puppet eyes, extending his clumsy, wire-pierced hands toward her. Elina leaned back slightly - soft, weightless, capable of the subtlest movements, both of body and soul. Finally, guided by the master's gentle touch, she surrendered to an unexpected joy. For the briefest of moments, she allowed herself to believe in this happiness, to plunge into its serene depths...

But the audience was restless. The lord's three children—the eldest imperious girl and two mischievous boys—whispered and fidgeted, threatening to ruin the performance. Yet by the time the final scene arrived, even they had quieted, mesmerized by Elina's portrayal. When the curtain fell, the girl lazily clapped her hands and declared with a haughty pout, "I want that doll for myself! How much does it cost?"

Elina froze, unsure how to respond. If the lord and her master struck a deal, she could be sold to this rich household—almost a castle! The mere thought made her head spin. Could it be? She, living in a palace, no longer just one among many, but if not the only, then one of the very few dolls—special, unique!

After her triumphant performance, she would surely become the children's favorite. They would cherish her, care for her as if she were more than just a doll—as if she were a living, breathing part of their family. They would tuck her in at night, sing her lullabies, and with the innocent spontaneity of children, show her the beauty of the world around them. And she, Elina, would respond in kind, offering them her softness and warmth, clinging to their hands as she once had clung to the puppeteer's, the hand that had given her life.

For a fleeting moment, the thought of leaving the theater brushed against her soul, stirring a faint, melancholy chill. But it quickly dissipated. In the theater, she had always been alone, misunderstood, just one among many—more fragile, more vulnerable, and, in her mind, more talented than the others. No matter how hard she tried, she never received the love she craved. But here, in this grand home, she would be loved simply for being herself, for bringing joy to the children with her very presence.

"Excellent, she's yours now," came the puppeteer's voice right next to her ear. "I hope your children will enjoy such a toy."

"I'm sure they will," the lord replied, taking Elina into his hands. "I have many exotic things, but I've never seen anything quite like this." With those words, he casually handed her to his daughter.

* * *

Elina glanced around, desperate and hounded. From her low vantage point on the floor, the already expansive two-story living room seemed even more vast and imposing. Though it was adorned with polished wood rather than the opulence of gold and marble, it still held an air of wealth. The varied shades of wood, ranging from deep burgundy to golden brown, lent the space a luxurious sheen. Every surface, every detail, boasted exquisite craftsmanship. The carvings that decorated the furniture and fixtures were fine and intricate, underscoring the rich elegance of the room.

High above, a carved balcony of light-colored wood ran along the second-floor wall, and from its railings, trophy heads of deer and mountain rams, their horns spiraled in elaborate curves, gazed down like sentinels. One particularly grand deer head loomed over the fireplace, its sprawling antlers extending along the wall, as though holding the room aloft with their ancient strength.

The dead eyes of the deer stared indifferently at the plush carpet and the imposing, yet comfortable, furniture. A solid writing desk stood near the fireplace, its legs also adorned with lavish carvings. Fresh flowers, recently arranged by a maid in an ornate vase, filled the air with their fragrance. Above, beneath a wood-paneled, triangular ceiling, hung a grand theater-like chandelier, strewn with dozens of candles.

Yet Elina had no time to marvel at the room's grandeur. She had only one thought: escape. The room was empty for now, and she frantically searched for a place to hide. Attempting to hide under the chairs or the desk was out of the question—the owner's dog would surely sniff her out. Her eyes fell on the bookcase near the fireplace, or more precisely, the narrow gap between it and the wall. It was a tight space, and Elina was afraid that her tiny weight would not be enough to push herself into the coveted gap. As she hesitated, a low, menacing bark echoed nearby, spurring her into action. In a surge of fear-driven strength, Elina managed to wedge herself between the wall and the bookcase, slipping through with surprising ease.

For what felt like the thousandth time in these dreadful weeks, she cursed her naive dreams and foolish ambitions.

The memory of her cozy puppet theater now shimmered like a lost paradise. The once-dull utility room, the chest she had loathed, now seemed like a sanctuary, and Elina despised herself for not realizing how truly content she had been. Peace, quiet, safety, and the reliable monotony of each day—what more could she have wished for? Yes, she had had her disappointments, her unmet dreams, but there had been joys too. She had performed on stage, among her fellow dolls, living in a world that, though not always perfect, was familiar and secure. And how could her small disappointments compare with the nightmare that she experienced here?

Now, she was alone, trapped in this hostile, glittering mansion. She had been right about one thing—she was indeed unique in the lord's house. There were no other soft toys here, only cold, cast-iron figurines and stiff clay dolls, incapable of even the slightest movement. These lifeless sculptures stared down from their shelves, mute witnesses to her suffering, and she knew they would never offer her sympathy or aid.

The children, however, had instantly recognized Elina's plasticity, but they had used it for their own cruel amusement. Fascinated by her unusual flexibility, they subjected her to merciless "games." The boys tied her delicate arms into knots, used her like a punching bag, and hung her from trees like some lifeless rag. Their sister, no kinder, jabbed pins into her, using her like a pillow for sewing practice. Elina, once an actress in a puppet theater, had never known such brutal attention. She would have given anything to escape such attention and never endure such treatment again.

But her suffering didn't end there. One day, after tiring of their games with her, the eldest boy suggested, "Let's give her to the dog. He'll love her—she's perfect for chewing on!"

Elina froze in horror, the world around her dissolving into a blur of dread. Her ears rang with disbelief—death was near, a brutal, agonizing death, in the savage maw of a beast. She could see it vividly: the Doberman, excited by the promise of fresh prey, sinking its fangs deeper into her flesh with every breath. She imagined its claws scraping restlessly across the cold floor, its powerful frame trembling in anticipation, the way it shook its head with a doll clenched between its jaws.

From that moment on, her life became a relentless game of cat and mouse, a constant flight from the monster eager to tear her apart. Each day brimmed with terror, every second driven by a singular aim—to survive. The Doberman was a looming shadow, vast, black, and fierce, the embodiment of some dark, devilish force. Even in the dog's absence, its presence haunted her. She could sense its breath on her skin, feel the tension coiling in every corner of that cursed house. Whenever she thought she had found a moment of safety, it would materialize, as if summoned by her very fear, its dark eyes gleaming, ready to spring.

Now, the beast prowled, whining low with hunger, pushing its muzzle against the narrow crevice where Elina had wedged herself. It was just as she had imagined—its claws raked the floor, its back arched, muscles taut with anticipation, ready to lunge at the coveted prey. The thrill of the hunt glimmered in the dog's eyes, mingling with an almost playful excitement. The taste of victory was so close it made the animal shiver, and it had no intention of giving up. Elina, seized with panic, squeezed further into the gap, but the beast's paw stretched closer, claws curling toward her, eager to catch hold.

And then, with a sudden burst of violence, the Doberman hurled itself forward, crashing its weight into the narrow space. The wardrobe trembled, its balance shifting precariously, until it began to tip—too slow, far too slow—onto the luxurious carpet. A shard of sunlight broke through the window, a beam like an arrow, illuminating the glossy black fur of the dog. Elina watched as joyful reflections darted across its sleek surface, and the dog, inspired by success, growled, triumphant, poised to claim its prize.

But before the beast could strike, a sharp voice shattered the moment. "What have you done, you stupid dog?" The owner's angry shout echoed above her. With a rough hand, he seized the Doberman by its collar, yanking it back from the wardrobe's edge. The dog whimpered, its mighty paws scrabbling against the floor in resistance, and Elina breathed a sigh of relief.

In that instant, the sheer force of her will to live surged through her, intoxicating and overwhelming. It was as though life itself rushed back into her veins, vibrant, electric, making her dizzy with its potency. She wanted to live, to breathe, to savor the texture of every moment, to bask in the beauty of existence, to feel its fullness with each of its threads, connecting the intricate patches of her fabric. The world seemed to explode with color—streams of light, movement of air, every fragment of reality flooded her senses, each second brimming with meaning, with purpose.

But bliss is fleeting.

"So, it was this rag you were after?" the owner muttered, his irritation palpable as he scooped Elina into his rough hand. "All that trouble for this? I spent all that money on you for what? Just for the dog to wreck my home over it?" With a sharp tug, he threw open the window, and before Elina could comprehend what was happening, he hurled her out into the yard.

"If that's your toy, you can play with it outside. No more chaos in my house," he scolded his pet. The Doberman whined shamefacedly and stood up, showing with all his appearance that he was ready to go outside at any moment.

Run. The thought shot through Elina's mind like a spark. Every fiber of her being thrummed with the desire to escape, to seize the life she had so desperately clung to moments before. How absurd it now seemed—that she had once squandered her existence in bitterness, in endless complaint, in the empty hope for miracles that never came. She had wasted so much time—time she could have spent living, breathing, feeling the warmth of the sun, smiling at the simple beauty of being alive. And now, all she wanted was to live. To exist, fully, deeply, and feel her involvement in everything that surrounded her.

The world itself seemed to fall into Elina's hands, wrapping around her with seductive ease, whispering its allure through scents, dazzling her with light, and caressing her with the gentle touch of a breeze. It approached her cautiously at first, playful, teasing, and feeling that she did not understand its hints, it acted more and more assertively, demanding her attention. It blinded her with sunlight, teased her with the approach of rain, and pounced on her with ragged gusts of wind. The world ached for her presence, begging her, minute by minute, to join in its rhythm, to partake in its untamed vitality. And now, at last, Elina answered its call.

She sprinted along the fence, her eyes scanning desperately for even the smallest crack in the towering stone wall. Finally, she reached the gate and, still not believing her luck, squeezed through the carved gap in the pattern of the lattice. Behind her, the Doberman had already leaped onto the lawn, its sleek body cutting across the grass with the lethal grace of a hunting beast. It surged forward like a bolt of lightning, relentless in its pursuit. At the gate, it skidded to a halt and howled, thrusting a paw between the iron bars in frustration.

Elina glanced back, her heart hammering in her chest. She turned and hurried away from the house—a place of luxury, but one that had become a waking nightmare. Ahead of her lay freedom—pure, unbounded freedom, a sensation so foreign to the fragile rag doll.

* * *

Elina walked down a sun-drenched street, where on either side rose mansions of extraordinary beauty. Each one, adorned with intricate woodwork or stone carvings, resembled a miniature palace, a testament to elegance and grandeur. The play of light and shadow danced across their facades, accentuating every delicate detail of their design. The graceful ornamentation of the cornices flowed seamlessly into the columns, and the fresh stonework of the facades complemented the open, inviting shutters.

On any other day, Elina might have been enchanted by the sheer beauty of these homes, her heart swelling with a childlike delight at their magnificence. She had always possessed that rare gift—the ability to take joy in the splendor of things that weren't hers, even fully aware of her own separation from such luxury.

Now, after all she had endured within such a house, the sight of these grand buildings filled Elina with a deep and visceral dread. To her, the stone walls and ornate stucco of the balconies concealed not beauty, but a hidden world of hypocrisy and cruelty, where mockery and malice festered behind gilded facades. The pristine exteriors, once a source of awe, now seemed to her nothing more than a mask, a false veneer covering the true ugliness of human nature. The more imposing and solid the house that rose before her, the more certain Elina became that evil lurked behind its doors.

The grand street of luxurious mansions gradually dissolved into more modest homes, their designs lighter, almost careless as if unburdened by the weight of wealth. These homes appeared simpler, and more welcoming, perhaps by that very carelessness. Children playing on the lawn here seemed kinder, the dogs that frolicked around them seemed more frivolous, amusing in their freedom.

Yet Elina—though once susceptible to the surface charm of such scenes—no longer allowed herself to be drawn in. Behind any, even the most innocent scene, she imagined the evil lurking in the depths of someone else's life. Like a black fog, insidious and pervasive, evil seeped from the cracks of even the happiest facades, poisoning the very air. And Elina pressed onward, fleeing from the deceptive warmth of others' joy as if their happiness itself were a curse. All she prayed for now was to remain unseen.

By evening, the city's heart began to reveal itself, its pulse harsher. The houses became smaller, shabbier, their once-private worlds laid bare to the streets, no longer shielded by high fences or carefully manicured lawns. They stood vulnerable, their facades cracked and worn, easily brushed against by the rushing passersby who seemed not to notice anything at all. Elina moved cautiously, close to the walls, slipping under the feet of people who hurried along, each consumed by their own private urgency. The streets became crowded, faces strained with purpose, strangers hurrying past without noticing anything around them. Among them, tourists lingered, eyes wide, capturing every detail as though fearing to miss a single note of the city's symphony.

But they were not what drew Elina's gaze. With her sensitive, artistic soul, she felt the pulse of loneliness that lingered in the air. It was an ache which she almost did not sense in the quiet green streets lined with opulent homes. Here, in the very heart of seething life, loneliness was palpable most vividly—woven into the very stones of the sidewalk, etched into the faces of the hurrying masses. The beggars she passed stared blankly into the void, dirty and ragged, and tried not to raise their eyes to passersby, gazing at the ground.

Turning the corner and cautiously peering out from behind it, Elina watched in surprise at how unhappy people truly were. From the stage, she had seen only their joyous faces, eager before the performance, radiant in their applause afterward. She remembered children, well-dressed and carefree, accompanied by their parents, whose expressions often bore the satisfied look of duty fulfilled. But here, amid the teeming life of the streets, bitterness and disappointment swirled like invisible currents. Resentment, pain, and misunderstanding drifted like smoke, much stronger than what Elina felt while sitting in her utility room.

And though a rare flicker of hope pierced the cold city air, it was swiftly extinguished, overwhelmed by the winds of loss. Yet the most powerful presence of all was indifference, vast and impenetrable. It clung to the buildings, settled into the cobblestones, and flowed from the very breath of those who passed by. It was cold, all-encompassing, transforming people into icy drifts that collided with one another without a thought. As the drizzle began, Elina felt the chill penetrate her very fibers, the dampness soaking through her fabric form. Desperate for shelter, she slipped unnoticed into the hotel restaurant and hid under the table.

The space was full, alive with voices and laughter, people gesturing and arguing, their drinks glinting under the warm light of the lamps. But Elina, with her finely tuned sense of human nature, could see what others might miss. Even here, in this oasis of seeming comfort, they were not truly escaping the rain. They were fleeing the loneliness that gnawed at them, leaping headlong into conversation as if diving off a cliff, as if the noise might drown out their isolation. They drank the wine, enjoying the way the joyful liquid spread through their veins, dulling their senses and offering them a fleeting sense of ease.

And as Elina watched, something inside her shifted. For the first time, she no longer looked at these towering figures with fear, but with pity. With their solid frames of muscle and bone, and not at all of soft, pliable pieces of fabric, they seemed as vulnerable as she was. Fragile, brittle, as if made of crystal, they banged thick glasses on the tables and bit with dog-like fury into the juicy flesh of the fried chicken served to them by the waiters. This gave them a sense of strength, as superficial and fragile as glass soaked with rainwater.

Elina had been so absorbed in watching the people around her that she didn't notice the swift hand of the young waiter as he scooped her up.

"Looks like one of the guests lost a doll," he remarked handing her over to the owner behind the counter with a casual toss.

The owner laughed, turning Elina in his hands with careless ease. "Look, she's got a hole at the bottom!" he chuckled, slipping her onto his hand. "We could put her on display—she'll brighten up the place for the guests."

With that, he perched Elina on a decorative fence that lined the interior of the restaurant. Now, instead of peering up at the people from below, she found herself at eye level with them, looking directly into their faces. Yet few took any real notice of her. Occasionally, someone would glance her way and offer a fleeting smile at the sight of the elegant doll, but mostly, they carried on, absorbed in their conversations. Strangely, Elina found herself warming to this new role. She became part of the atmosphere, lending a sense of warmth and homeliness to the space. The guests seemed to relax in her presence, their voices softening as they shared their stories and laughter.

They were no longer grateful spectators—the public from whom Elina had once sought delight and recognition, though she had always regarded them with a certain indulgence as if they were merely an audience upon which she could unfold the brilliance of her singular talent. Nor were they the capricious rulers of her fate, cruel and unpredictable, whose slightest gesture or most trivial action she had once awaited, like a beggar for a handout, knowing it could irrevocably alter the course of her life. Now, they stood before her, laid bare in their complete and candid humanness, vulnerable as she was.

There was, for instance, the old gambler who frequented the place each evening to best his friend at cards. Elina had come to learn that he had a daughter he had not seen in years, a daughter who had never forgiven him for abandoning their family long ago. At another table, a mother and her young daughter sat, the very image of ordinary tourists. Yet, Elina had overheard the mother, inquiring with quiet desperation at the reception desk if there were any letters addressed to her, as though she awaited something—or perhaps, fled from something. Elina did not know the full story, but she instinctively recognized the signs. This was not just a holiday. It was an escape, just as Elina herself had once fled—from one nightmare into the frightening unknown of another.

How ironic, she thought, that people envied one another without ever truly knowing what lay behind the façade now laid bare before her. She understood now, more deeply than ever, that human destiny was not something to be envied. The lives of others, with their intricate and unspoken tragedies, often eclipsed the most skillful narratives of a playwright.

Meeting after meeting, departure after departure, hopes kindled and dashed, dreams clashing against the cold walls of reality—these stories flowed endlessly past Elina's eyes, unwittingly divulged by those living them. And somehow, she felt their pain with more intensity than her own. Immersed in the kaleidoscope of humanity, she dissolved into its current, growing accustomed to her new role—the hospitable hostess.

After all, it was her hotel that, however briefly, sheltered those in search of refuge. For travelers, it was a gateway to a city of vibrant colors and new experiences. For fugitives, it became a hiding place. For lovers, it offered moments of short pleasure. And for everyone, without exception, it provided a soft bed and a roof overhead, a sanctuary as essential as it was fleeting. Elina found a quiet joy in the role, imagining herself the owner of the hotel, offering solace to every traveler who crossed her threshold.

But her illusions did not last long. One day, she noticed a ragged beggar girl lingering near the door of the hotel lobby. Through the open doorway of the restaurant, she watched as the doorman, with casual cruelty, seized the girl by the scruff of her neck and tossed her into the street. Elina's heart clenched at the sight, but she felt powerless to intervene. She gazed through the restaurant window at the girl, now pressed against the glass, and only the raindrops cut through the frozen glass surface between them in wavy paths.

It was not the last time Elina saw her. More than once, the girl managed to sneak into the restaurant, usually accompanied by an older brother. When he distracted the doorman, the girl would slip inside and sit quietly in a corner, her eyes hungrily following the diners. Sometimes, one of them would take pity on her, offering her a cake or a drink. She would seize the treat gratefully, wrap it in whatever scrap of paper she had, and rush out to share it with her brother. More often, though, she was unceremoniously thrown out before she could taste anything. Then, again she would dawdle sadly outside the window, looking at the counter.

On this day, everything unfolded as it always had. Elina stood tall over the fence, while a girl huddled in the corner, nibbling on a piece of pie left by a previous patron. Suddenly, the waiter's sharp eyes fell upon her.

"What are you doing here, beggar?" he barked, his voice a whip of anger as he lunged to seize the girl by the sleeve. "What have you stolen, you little thief?"

The girl leaped to her feet, slipping from his grasp like a hunted wolf cub, crashing into the ornamental fence in her way. At that instant, it felt to Elina as though the ground beneath her gave way, sending her downward. She spun through the air in a helpless pirouette and landed at the restaurant's threshold. The girl, quick as a flash, vaulted over her prone form, and the enraged waiter stormed after her, his fury palpable. As he thundered past, Elina was seized by a bright memory—herself, fleeing in terror from a snarling dog. Almost before she realized what she was doing, she flung herself at his feet, causing him to sprawl across the threshold like a hotel rug.

"Worthless rag!" he spat, grabbing Elina. In a fit of temper, he hurled her through the open hotel door after the fleeing girl. The doorman, swift in his duties, swung the heavy door shut, leaving Elina discarded once more on the street—this time, face to face with the girl she had unwittingly followed. Fear coiled tight in Elina's chest at the thought of being swept up by human hands once again, but it was too late. The girl bent down, tenderly lifting the abandoned doll from the dirt.

"They threw you out too, didn't they?" she asked, her voice laced with sympathy. "Don't worry, we'll survive together now."

* * *

It was cold and damp beneath the bridge, though the river it spanned had shrunk to a mere trickle, rendering the once-mighty structure more decorative than functional. At the foot of the bridge, a small niche had been carved into the stone, and it was here, in this shallow recess, that two homeless orphans—a brother and sister—had made their fragile home. The bridge and its stone hollow shielded them from the rain and, to some degree, from the biting wind, but neither could keep out the persistent chill or the creeping moisture. The cardboard boxes they had scavenged and the threadbare rags spread over the boards beneath them offered little protection from the elements.

Elina, the doll who had once graced a warm puppet theater and later adorned the entrance to a restaurant, was now plunged into an existence of utter destitution. It seemed that the main law of life she had learned in that dim storage room had once again proven itself. Gone were the bright lights and admiring gazes of an audience; gone even were the bustling secrets of the restaurant where human fates seemed to unravel before her eyes. Now, she found herself on the very edge of existence, cast aside into a world so impoverished and bleak that even the most wretched souls avoided it. In the ceaseless damp beside the stagnant stream, Elina could feel her fabric swelling with moisture, growing heavy and giving her an unfamiliar heft.

Yet, this discomfort was of little concern to her now. What mattered more, far more, was that for the first time, Elina was not alone in her plight. She had learned that her new owner's name was Olivia, and her brother, Jacob. Together, she and Olivia embarked on daily searches for food, a task as daunting as necessary. Olivia often lingered behind taverns, hoping for the kindness of maids who might spare a scrap or two. At other times, she begged at the entrance to the railway station, her small figure nearly lost in the constant flow of hurried travelers, all of them too preoccupied with their own lives.

Elina had come to understand how many burdens, worries, and concealed sorrows lay behind their ostentatious composure and imaginary well-being. The travelers rushed past, deliberately avoiding Olivia's gaze, their faces averted in feigned concentration. Sometimes, Olivia returned to their shelter empty-handed, the gnawing hunger in her belly unrelieved. Unlike her brother, however, she never dared to steal.

Jacob, though, had no such reservations. Feeling the weight of responsibility for his sister, he often took greater risks, determined to find food by any means. It was not unusual for him to dart through the crowded streets, evading the grip of burly, mustachioed gentlemen or the swift feet of policemen. In such moments of danger, Jacob never led his pursuers back to the bridge. Instead, he wove through the maze of city streets, drawing the chase far from their fragile refuge. Elina had no doubt: young Jacob's love for his sister was sincere.

Love—pure, unguarded love—was what Elina felt in every fiber of her being within this strange family of children. Olivia loved her brother with tenderness and selflessness, and she also loved Elina. Here, in the cold, weather-beaten half-room, half-gateway, sheltered from the outside world only by stone ledges and a flimsy plywood partition, the rag doll's wildest dreams had come true. Each night, Olivia curled up on her makeshift bed, trembling from the cold, and held Elina close, tighter than any pillow, seeking warmth. And Elina, in her own silent way, embraced the girl back, wishing she could truly warm her with her softness.

Olivia had never seen Elina perform on stage. In her brief and challenging life, she had never set foot in a theater and had no inkling of the hidden talents of her newfound doll. Yet she loved Elina simply, unconditionally, and artlessly—she loved her for being there, for existing. It was a love so pure that Elina struggled to believe it. Could it be possible that someone would cherish her without knowing her worth, without seeing her perform, without recognizing her talents? The thought seemed too miraculous to comprehend.

For a long time, Olivia hadn't even noticed the slit in Elina's lower half, the small opening meant for a puppeteer's hand. And when she finally did, she didn't understand its purpose.

"Look," she said, showing the discovery to her brother, "you can keep treasures inside my doll—the most precious ones. No one will find them here!"

With that, she carefully tucked a tiny medallion into Elina—a medallion that held photographs of her and Jacob's long-lost parents. Olivia pushed it deep inside the doll's fabric, right where a heart would be. Elina couldn't believe her fortune. For the first time in her life, she possessed something other dolls had—a heart, a solid, real heart. It became her anchor, her foundation. The thought alone gave her an unfamiliar strength, as if the tiny medallion had transformed her, threading her entire body with a new resilience, like an invisible wire frame.

"Wait, it can be used for something better than hiding things," Jacob interjected. "It's for putting the doll on your hand. Watch!" With a grin, he slipped his hand into the rag doll and playfully swiveled her from side to side.

"We can make money with this!" he exclaimed, excitement lighting up his face. "If we perform with her in the squares, people will give us more than they do now. We just need to give her a name."

"Mary?" Olivia suggested quietly. "Let's call her Mary."

"Hi, I'm Mary!" Jacob chimed in, mimicking a girl's voice as he twirled Elina toward his sister.

"Let me try," Olivia said, gently taking the doll from her brother's hand. She began to play with Elina—hesitant, awkward, her movements shy and uncertain. Elina could sense Olivia's every hesitation, every faltering motion. It had been so long since Elina had felt a hand guiding her, and she had longed for it. But Olivia's hand was not the commanding, confident hand of a seasoned puppeteer. It didn't imbue Elina with life, didn't awaken her talents, didn't help her believe in herself, even for a moment. Olivia's hand was timid, fumbling for the right gesture, unsure of how to lead. She stood before Elina not as a master of the doll, but as someone seeking her approval, her silent support.

Elina had never considered taking the lead, never imagined playing a role greater than that of an object controlled by another's hand. But something had shifted inside her—perhaps it was the weight of the medallion resting where her heart now lay, or perhaps it was the love she felt for Olivia, and the deep worry that her young mistress would falter, unable to earn the money she and Jacob so desperately needed to survive.

And so, with a quiet, almost imperceptible movement, Elina began to guide Olivia's hand—gently, at some hidden level, shaping the performance. No longer could she surrender fully to her puppeteer's will, as she once had. Now, Elina reached out in her own subtle way, feeling for the character, hoping to impart it to Olivia. From somewhere deep, as if from the very fabric of the universe, from the dampness suspended in the air, from the dirty blankets strewn over bare boards, Elina summoned her greatest creation—her most wondrous role. She could not say where this newfound strength came from, but with each tentative gesture Olivia made, Elina's own movements grew more assured, the flow of the game clearer and more certain.

Olivia seemed to sense the doll's subtle guidance and began to adjust to it, timidly at first, then with growing confidence. As the minutes passed, the girl became more absorbed, swept away by the magic of the performance. With childlike spontaneity and an almost adult-like dedication, Olivia surrendered to the enchantment of their shared creation. It was no longer just Olivia's game—it had become a partnership, an unrivaled duet of human and doll. And for the first time, Elina played the leading role. With the wisdom of a seasoned mentor, she guided Olivia's hand, opening the doorway to a magical world of storytelling.

"Are you sure you can do it?" Jacob asked, his voice tinged with doubt.

"I'm sure!" Olivia answered, her voice ringing with new-found certainty.

Their premiere came the next morning, on the cold, gray stones of the station square. There were no stage lights, no warm theater seats, no velvet curtains to set the scene. Olivia crouched on the frigid pavement, performing her first puppet show. The passersby bustled past in their hurried routines, but slowly, some began to stop, casting curious glances at the girl and her doll. Most paused only briefly, checking the time on the grand clocktower before rushing off to catch their trains. But inevitably, a few lingered, drawn in by the simple tale Olivia was unfolding, captivated by the delicate movements of the doll in her hands.

For Elina, the performance had never meant as much as it did now. She poured all her pliability, her softness, her very fragility into the act, and strangely, these qualities—once her vulnerabilities—now became her source of strength. It felt to Elina as if an invisible radiance poured from the cobblestones around them, like sunlight, warming the cold and banishing the loneliness that had thickened around them. The light grew stronger, and as if sensing it, more and more people gathered, watching in awe. Soon, coins began to ring as they hit the stones, their sound mixing with the laughter and applause of the growing crowd. But neither the girl nor the doll paid any attention to the clinking of money; they continued to play, giving birth to ever more marvelous images, in perfect unity.

It was a success—greater than Elina could have ever imagined, even in her most fanciful dreams. The sun's golden light reflected off the scattered coins, glinting on the faces of the onlookers, spreading smiles. The very space around them seemed to come alive, awakened by those smiles.

"I didn't know you were such a wonderful actress," Olivia whispered softly to Elina, her voice filled with awe.

"You are the actress," Elina thought in reply. "I'm just helping you discover that."

As Elina gazed at the streams of sunlight and the gold coins scattered along the pavement, she realized that she would never trade her greatest treasure—the sense of human hands that held her, warming her from the inside—for anything in the world.

A Tale of Stardust

MANUEL REVERENTLY TOUCHED THE REMAINS of the ancient brick wall. Despite the passage of thousands of years, its masonry, corroded by time, remained impressively distinct. Though broken at the edges and pocked with potholes and cracks, with tufts of sun-bleached grass sprouting in places, the wall still withstood the relentless march of centuries. Manuel could discern in the still air a special, barely perceptible breath—the breath of time.

From these massive relics of the past, all that now remained were the windswept contours of semicircular arches. Once, these arches had gazed with their black eye sockets into the depths of magnificent Roman palaces, symbols of the empire's boundless power. Now, torn from their era and deprived of their original supports, they stood in an open field, bathed in sunlight and buffeted by winds, like gates leading to nowhere. Yet, seemingly rooted in the very foundations of the earth, these walls continued to stubbornly stand as an eternal reminder of ancient civilizations.

Manuel was not interested in how many generations' blood had soaked the ground at his feet. He listened instead to a different music—the sweetest vibration for him—the pulsation of time flowing through the ages. Over millennia, this unique essence, beyond human control, had nourished the stones so completely that it seemed they were imbued with all the strength of accumulated time. In his years of wandering, Manuel had learned to sense this unmistakably, and now, reverently pausing for a moment, he bowed to the ground at the very foot of the ancient ruins.

He was not mistaken—a thin layer of gold dust covered the wind-polished clay. Taking out a precious vessel hidden at his chest, Manuel carefully opened the lid. A thin stream of golden sand soared into the air, obediently crawling into the opened hole like a genie returning to its lamp. Barely noticeable plumes of dust now floated into his vessel not only from the ground but also from the time-worn bricks of ancient Roman buildings, flowing into it like golden threads.

Manuel said a silent prayer as he watched the shimmering stream, hoping it would continue as long as possible. The ruins, frozen in eternal immobility, calmly observed as sparkling specks of dust slowly drifted through the air, reflecting the sunlight. Having endured countless destructions and wars, having felt the boundless greatness and deep decline, having vanished into oblivion and yet still remaining alive, they did not notice this loss, just as they were accustomed to not noticing any other losses. It seemed that eternity itself, entangled in the remains of stone labyrinths, had settled and spilled over the earth, imparting part of its immortality to transient matter.

"Did you find it?" a quiet voice asked right next to his ear. Manuel turned and saw the commandant—immaculate as always in his perfectly fitting uniform, hovering slightly above the earth's surface. Manuel had long ago grown accustomed to his commandant's habit of standing a meter above the ground, as if he disdained touching it with his soles.

"There's very little here," Manuel replied. "But there are other ruins ahead, so there is hope of discovering new sources. Excavations have already begun at the previous site, and now you won't find even a grain of sand there. Tours will start soon, which means that we have nothing to hope for."

"Damned people!" the commandant's eyes flashed angrily. "They can't use it; they don't even see it! Not only do they receive it so much and squander it wastefully, but in their ignorance, they destroy the last reserves where it can still be found..." Interrupting himself, he turned to Manuel. "Three of them, a so-called 'illegal expedition', are heading here. You know they will ruin everything just by being here."

"When will they arrive?" Manuel asked, turning pale. "I need a few more days to collect everything."

"They should be here tomorrow," the commandant said angrily. "That's why I wanted to warn you. This must not be allowed to happen."

"Will you take care of them?" Manuel asked hopefully.

"No," the commandant snapped. "There are only three; you can handle them yourself."

"Are you sure?" Manuel asked hesitantly, not looking forward to the task.

"This is an order," the commandant answered harshly. "You know what needs to be done."

He disappeared, as usual, by dissolving into the air. Manuel sighed, hiding the precious vessel at his chest and bowing to the ground—the same ground where, until recently, golden grains of sand invisible to ordinary eyes had sparkled. Slowly, with practiced movements, Manuel placed his hands on the surface and sent a clear and strong vibration deep into the earth. In response, the earth trembled, filling with an even hum. Manuel waited, patiently kneeling and keeping his hands pressed to the heated clay.

Soon, his efforts were rewarded. Responding to his call, snakes emerged from the ground. Wriggling in time with the surface's vibrations, they slithered towards him, hissing and flicking their forked tongues. Manuel looked at them without the slightest fear, his hands still pressed to the now almost hot ground. Their ominous silent dialogue continued for several minutes. Finally, the snakes obediently bowed to him and began to crawl away in small, nimble zigzags, disappearing into the burnt grass.

* * *

Estherita gathered her strength and took a few more steps up the steep serpentine road. Her efforts were rewarded. The forested mountain slopes and a gentle incline, like a verdant carpet, spread out before her. Red mountain poppies, scattered like rubies, dotted the hills, as if the earth's blood had surfaced. Below, where the plain began, the scars of ancient fortress walls were visible against the green backdrop. Most of the walls now lay deep underground, and only the low, ragged stonework was visible above. Its surface, marred by potholes and cracks, was now helplessly bristling with the sharp corners of broken bricks breaking through the moss.

"We'll have to dig a lot here," Gilberto said disappointedly, following her gaze.

"Not that much," Christian tried to reassure him. "Archaeologists have told me more than once that they found fragments of pottery directly in the masonry of the walls. You'd be surprised how many valuable things can be found in these ruins. Don't forget: there was once a city here, and ordinary people lived in it. Throughout this entire territory..." he waved his hand vaguely, pointing to the plain beneath them. "This entire space was built up. Start digging anywhere, and you'll come across the remains of their houses. And every Roman, without exception, had simple utensils, which today are priceless. Imagine if we excavate the imperial palace!" His eyes sparkled greedily.

Estherita saw how Christian's enthusiasm rubbed off on Gilberto. Strangely, she did not feel any greedy anticipation at all. Of course, it would be tempting to hold the luxurious jewelry that once adorned the wives of Roman Caesars, now dull from time, soaked in the earth, rough from the sand that had grown into them. But Estherita was thinking of something else. In place of the green and red carpet of poppy fields, she imagined bustling city streets. On both sides rose massive, reliable houses made of light stone. People jostled between them, hurrying to the city square where visiting merchants briskly conducted trade.

Nobles walked slowly to the huge baths, where all the social life of that time thrived. Leaving wet footprints on the stone slabs, they emerged from the water and sat near the huge columns—as tall as if they supported the sky itself. Everything here seemed monumental, unshakable, impervious to any human or natural elements. Rome reigned over the planet, so that the sun itself rose into the sky only to illuminate Caesar's greatness. This city symbolized immortality, and now its pitiful remains timidly emerged from beneath the earth with uneven, broken edges.

A profound sense of futility and the insignificance of human life crystallized in Estherita's mind, prompting her to look around helplessly. It seemed as if it was not the mountains and forests that surrounded her, but time itself, advancing upon their small group with the same insidious intent that had once approached this seemingly invincible city, reducing it almost to the ground.

"All this splendor began to be built in the first century, and by the fifth, it was destroyed by the Huns," Christian said. He tried to maintain a calm demeanor, but to Estherita, his voice carried a subtle note of melancholy in the face of inexorable decay.

"They would have perished anyway, even without the Huns," Gilberto shrugged. "We too will be nothing but remnants in these stones one day, turning to ashes and dust, because no one is exempt," he added philosophically.

"Why don't we set up camp?" Christian suggested, clearly eager to steer the conversation away from the grim subject of mortality. They began to build a fire atop the hill, and Estherita was relieved that, once she sat on the grass, the plain, scarred by Roman ruins, was hidden from view by the mountain's edge. Now, a soft carpet of grass spread around her, dotted with red flowers as if scattered from the sky. Nature enveloped them, caressing their eyes with its beauty, beckoning with inaccessible mountain peaks, and lulling them with a bluish haze descending from the clouds. The clouds and the forests seemed to flow towards their feet, close and welcoming, enveloping them in peace.

A breeze stirred, and Christian gently placed a shawl over her shoulders. Estherita felt a sudden, amazing happiness. Amidst recent troubles, she had forgotten what such happiness felt like, and now she tried to embrace this fragile feeling, etching into her memory the flower-strewn carpet, the mountain slopes, and the hand of a loved one on her shoulder. How she wished to freeze this moment, stretching it into eternity, making it a constant, immutable presence in her life.

The fire began to flare up, its flames flirting with the wind, dancing in the air and warming it with a quivering heat. Estherita nestled closer to Christian, feeling a slight pang of fear. She dreaded losing him, a prospect that had nearly come to pass when her father, enraged and out of control, had shouted:

"I'll lock him up, do you hear? This rogue will end his life behind bars. Never go near him again!"

Estherita shuddered. The bliss that had enveloped her vanished without a trace, replaced once more by anxiety—the constant companion of her life in recent weeks. Never before had she seen her father so fanatically adamant, transformed entirely into a vessel of hatred—hatred toward her lover. Estherita knew her father was hot-tempered, but she could never have imagined he would stoop to such malice—to imprison an innocent man just to keep him from seeing his daughter.

Christian was innocent—of this Estherita was utterly convinced. The man now holding her by the shoulders, whose boundless tenderness was evident even in such a simple and tender gesture, simply could not be a cold-blooded robber. Even their current decision to profit from the remains of the ancient Roman city was not easy for him—Estherita was certain of it.

"It's not even theft, we're just trying to find the treasure. People who died more than one and a half thousand years ago will definitely have no use for their possessions, but for us, this could be a chance for a new life," he reassured her, though it seemed to Estherita that he was trying to convince himself as much as her.

Estherita could not abandon the cherished hope that simple human happiness awaited her and Christian. They would find ancient Roman artifacts and escape forever, making their way through the forests and plains to another country, where they could sell their discoveries and live in wealth and happiness.

"How long does it take to walk from here to the nearest village?" she asked Christian, peering into the distance.

"According to my calculations, we should reach it within 24 hours," he responded.

"The village is good," Gilberto interjected. "But we need to get to the nearest town, and the sooner the better."

"In any case, finding buyers for our finds will not be a quick task," Christian reasoned.

"I'm not talking about the finds," Gilberto waved him off. "I'd like to get to the telegraph office as quickly as possible to tell my aunt that I'm okay."

"Make sure your aunt doesn't give us away," Christian warned, alarmed.

"I already told you, she is absolutely reliable and will remain silent as a fish," Gilberto assured him. "Maybe your families have a custom to destroy relatives, but mine doesn't and I'm not going to cut off ties with people I love. Besides, no one knows that I left with you, and my telegram won't help the police find you."

"Do you think the police are already looking for us?" Estherita glanced at Christian, alarmed.

"I don't know," he turned to the fire, trying to conceal his anxiety. "Your father was determined. I'm afraid he might have them send officers after us."

"But they can't act solely on his words," Estherita tried to reason. "Without any evidence, they can't arrest you."

"Don't forget how influential your father is," Christian countered. "He has the power to fabricate evidence or convince the court it exists out of nothing."

Estherita lowered her head, dejected. She wanted him to reassure her, even though she understood that certain things were beyond Christian's control. An ominous future loomed ever clearer before her, obscuring the wooded mountain slopes, the bowls of blossoming poppies, and the gentle play of the breeze. Wind and fire surrounded her, caressing her with warmth and invigorating freshness, yet she no longer noticed anything around her.

"Okay, I'll take a walk. I won't disturb you," Gilberto finally said, breaking the awkward silence. He, too, seemed preoccupied with something.

"My friend, there is no telegraph here," Christian attempted to joke, but Gilberto merely smiled wryly and walked towards a small grove nestled behind the mountain ledge. Left alone, Estherita once again felt the ease and comfort of being near Christian. She even found solace in sitting beside him in silence, sharing in their mutual anxiety and relishing the moments that belonged to them alone.

Time united them—two such different people—granting them a fleeting yet profound sense of unity, an extraordinary feeling of togetherness, and the joy of closeness. Estherita watched in fascination the almost magical way everything around them seemed to divide into two yet multiply, expanding and merging with them in the unity of the moment. It felt as if, with just a bit more effort, she would catch its pulse and dissolve in the bliss of the present moment.

Just then an ominous hissing pierced her reverie. From the soft grass, as if oozing from the very heart of the earth, snakes slithered towards her feet. Black, golden, spotted, and some shimmering with a bluish glow, they wriggled, flicking their tongues menacingly. One snake, striped like a tiger in black and yellow, unceremoniously crawled into her lap and, arching, raised its head to face her. Its eyes locked onto hers, drawing her into an endless kaleidoscope of a parallel reality, as deep as the universe itself.

Silent horror gripped Estherita as she watched the snakes' coils entangle her arms and legs: cold, sliding over her skin with their elastic scales, inexorable in every movement. They continued to emerge from the ground like the tentacles of an invisible octopus: predatory, yellow-eyed, poised to tear their prey apart at any moment. Estherita turned to Christian and saw that he, too, was entwined with snakes from head to toe.

"Don't move," he whispered, but Estherita was already holding her breath in fear. The snakes' bodies, tense as if ready to strike at any moment, pinned her to the ground, preventing her from moving. Trembling, she braced herself for a painful death, but the snakes seemed to hesitate. They appeared to relish their power over the helpless prey, in no hurry to kill but also not intending to release her.

Estherita raised her eyes to the mountain ledge and saw Gilberto's face, pale with horror. He stood motionless for a moment, then, stumbling awkwardly, he turned and ran down the slope.

* * *

The interior of the inn was deliberately unpretentious: bare, uneven walls not even covered with plaster, rough wooden tables that looked as if they had been hastily hewn from single pieces of wood, and a plank floor stained from spilled booze. Only the wall behind the stage was carefully paneled with expensive wood, against which the musicians strained, their voices muffled by the roar of the music. The visitors relaxed and sipped their beer, enjoying the pleasant twilight of the tavern and the singing from the stage.

Perhaps, in this entire place, only Gilberto could not relax, though he had already drunk quite a lot. He stared blankly at his half-empty glass, repeating one phrase as if wound up:

"It was like some kind of Egyptian plague; it seemed as if all the snakes on the planet had crawled there and attacked them. A terrible sight. I must inform the count, Estherita's father, about everything."

"Don't even think about it!" his companion jumped up, pouring himself whiskey. "What will that bring you other than trouble? We agreed on everything in advance: you would tell the count where his daughter and her lover are only after we get to the ancient Roman treasures with their help. There is a completely understandable logic in this—then everything will go to us. Christian will deal with the police, and his girlfriend will have no time for ancient trinkets. In that case, the count would be grateful to you. But imagine how he would react if you told him that his daughter, along with this bandit, died in some distant mountains from the bites of poisonous snakes?"

"Of course, he will be heartbroken. That's natural," Gilberto responded. "But this does not mean we should hide from him how his daughter died."

"Understand, it's not about them now," the companion explained. "If she's dead, you can't help her. But imagine how many questions the count will have about what exactly you did with them in this wilderness and why you didn't tell him earlier where to find them? If his daughter were alive, he'd be too glad to have found her and wouldn't think about such trifles. But now that she's gone, His Highness will actively seek those responsible for her death, and you will be the main suspect. The count will accuse you of not saving her and will ask how you ended up with them. And what is this all for? We never got to the treasure!" he said with annoyance.

"All you can think about are those Roman trinkets!" Gilberto said, refilling his glass to the brim. "Antonio, if you're not afraid of snakes, you could go there now."

"I would have gone there long ago if I knew exactly where this damn Roman city was located!" Antonio retorted. "Why do you think we needed Christian? You've been pretending to be his friend all this time just because he had a map of those ruins."

"Christian really did consider me a friend, by the way," Gilberto responded dully. "He always believed in me and couldn't imagine that I was going to betray him."

"Don't get caught up in the pangs of conscience now," Antonio interrupted. "Your Christian was far from an angel. He could play the innocent lamb in front of his Estherita, making her believe her cruel father wanted to destroy him, but he never admitted to her that he was actually a thief. He tactfully remained silent when her father said that he belonged in prison. He started dating Estherita to gain access to her money, and only then supposedly fell in love with her—supposedly, because we don't know this for sure. You would have done a good deed if you had turned them into the police. And for this good deed, we would have received a small reward in the form of some unfortunate Roman figurines."

"I already told you, if you want, we can go there right now," Gilberto replied dully, staring at the glass again. "We don't need a map anymore; I remember the road by heart. We had almost reached the remains of the ancient city. From where we stood, the fortress walls were visible. We can go there again if you're so impatient, though if it were up to me, I wouldn't go near that damned place again."

"So why were you silent before!" Antonio jumped up. "It's already night, but tomorrow at dawn, we'll head there."

"On one condition," Gilberto raised his index finger into the air, as if hoping to find support for his body, losing stability from the whiskey. "After we find your treasure, I will tell the count where his daughter is. We can say that you and I went to wander through the forests and discovered them by accident. Then there will be no questions for us."

"I don't know," Antonio said hesitantly, setting aside the nearly empty bottle. "It's better, of course, not to draw attention to us or this place at all. And you know we can't help the dead."

"I told you my conditions," Gilberto answered firmly, with drunken intensity. "And anyway, where did you get the idea that they were dead? When I left, both were still alive. What if the snakes didn't touch them?"

"I wouldn't count on it," Antonio responded doubtfully. "More than a day has passed. In any case, we need to get to bed now. Tomorrow at dawn, we will go to your magic city."

* * *

The morning greeted them with predawn freshness, signaling a clear and hot day ahead. The forest welcomed the friends with lush greenery, laying a soft grass carpet under their feet, only occasionally tinged with the sun-scorched yellow at the edges. They walked all day, and only by evening did they finally reach the plain where the remains of an ancient civilization lay beneath the thickness of the earth. Dusk crept down from the mountains, clinging to tree branches and slowly filling the forest, gradually consuming the remnants of daylight.

At last, the forest ended, and between the treasure hunters and the Roman ruins lay only a small open space, gently undulating with the line of the hill. The scars of the ancient walls stood out with their ragged edges against the rapidly darkening sky. Suddenly, Antonio grabbed Gilberto by the hand and pulled him back toward the low trees at the edge of the plain.

"What is that?" Antonio whispered in fear, bending down. Gilberto instinctively clung to the tree, frantically looking at his feet, dreading the sight of deadly snakes in the encroaching darkness.

"No, over there," Antonio interrupted him, pointing toward the ruins of the ancient city. Peering closer, Gilberto saw a short human figure in a strange golden suit. The unusual guest knelt at the remains of the wall and carefully opened something that looked like a bottle of perfume or a vial of pharmaceutical potions. Before their amazed eyes, a thin stream of golden pollen floated into the air from the ancient stones. It spread like a lunar path in weightlessness, flowing smoothly into the bottle.

Not believing the miracle unfolding before him, Gilberto rubbed his eyes. The moonlight reflected in the golden stream, intensifying its radiant sparkle. He glanced at Antonio, who, frozen, also stared at the stream of stardust. Instinctively, Gilberto leaned forward to examine the unusual sight more closely when the stardust began to melt and dry up before their eyes, not reaching the bottle.

The alarmed little man sank to the ground, as if hoping to find an answer there. Then, realizing something, he turned sharply in their direction. His face was as golden as his suit, glowing in the moonlight just like the golden trickle they had just seen. His eyes sparkled with a bright blue flash, illuminating the entire space around them.

"You?" he said angrily, noticing Antonio and Gilberto. "How did you end up here? Even the commandant didn't notice you. Why are you all crawling here like locusts? Wasn't yesterday's lesson enough for you?" He moved menacingly towards them.

Antonio was the first to react and began to run, colliding with trees in his panic. Gilberto, as if petrified, froze, staring at the stranger. It seemed to him that the golden man had broken away from the surface of the earth and was floating above it. The stranger's words felt like a harbinger of imminent death, and a terrible guess dawned on Gilberto. Of course, it was this strange creature that had set the snakes on his companions! Horror mingled strangely with hope in Gilberto's heart. He suddenly realized that fleeing from this powerful creature was pointless. However, he still had a small chance to talk to the stranger and somehow try to beg for mercy.

"Please, we will not harm you," Gilberto muttered, stepping out from behind the tree and raising his hands in a gesture of helplessness. The golden man was now standing directly in front of him. He looked almost like any other person, but he was slightly shorter, and the golden hue of his face resembled a mask.

"You have already harmed us," the stranger snapped. "You caused irreparable harm. You destroyed this place."

"But we didn't even touch it!" Gilberto protested hotly. "This is the second time we haven't even managed to reach it."

"You got close enough to destroy the stardust," the stranger retorted. "Just because you can't see it doesn't mean you can't consume it."

"Consume?" Gilberto responded in shock. "But how exactly?"

"With your presence," the stranger said bitterly. "Do you know what stardust is? It's time. With your fear, your running around, your bustle, your very lives, you consume it every second, and no matter how much is given to you, you always want more."

"Time?" Gilberto asked, confused, slowly lowering his hands. "But time passes equally for all living beings, and no one can consume it more than others."

"It only seems that way to you," the golden guest smiled bitterly. His anger began to fade, giving way to sadness. "My name is Manuel, and I came here from a distant planet," he began. "Once upon a time, a terrible tragedy happened in our homeland—the flow of time was disrupted."

"So you can be in the past and the future?" Gilberto asked in surprise, with notes of envy in his voice.

"Do you think it's a fascinating journey through different eras?" Manuel grinned contemptuously. "In reality, it's constant chaos and an inability to exist normally, let alone be happy. We cannot feel the present and enjoy the current moment."

"It's very difficult to feel the present in general," Gilberto awkwardly tried to console him. "It is elusive and so fleeting that it's impossible to grasp. Every moment instantly becomes the past, and the future, though seemingly close, never arrives. It's impossible to catch up it."

"You just don't understand how much you've been given," Manuel responded, and there was undisguised envy in his voice. "Every second of your life, you live in the present and can experience it fully. For us, life has turned into constant torture. We try to take a step and hit a wall because we suddenly find ourselves in a past that cannot be changed. We try to enjoy the current moment, but the moment begins to dissolve around us because it turns out to be a future that doesn't yet exist. Everything that surrounds us in such a moment is a mirage. As soon as something worthwhile appears in our life, time shifts again, and we lose what is dear to us. Those we considered close no longer remember us. The entire course of life is disrupted, and we not only cannot plan anything but cannot even exist normally."

"Wow!" Gilberto whistled. "That is real torture. How did such an awful thing happen to you?"

"If we knew, don't you think we would have tried to fix it?" Manuel answered angrily. "Perhaps our ability to transmit our will to all living beings through vibrations disrupted the gravity of our planet, or maybe the movement of satellites in its orbit is to blame—who knows? Our best scientists are working tirelessly to solve this problem. But the continuation of their work without the normal flow of time is also impossible."

"And what can be done about it?" Gilberto asked, bewildered.

"We found a way out," Manuel replied, his voice growing muffled as if he were sharing his most cherished secret and feared it might be overheard, though there was not a soul around. "We discovered that time flows differently on your planet," he said in a solemn half-whisper.

"Differently?" Gilberto asked in astonishment. "That can't be!"

"The movement of the Earth is gradually accelerating," Manuel explained patiently. "And human life accelerates even more. You live in such a bustle, in such a rush, that you devour all the time allotted to you without a trace, often wasting it in vain. But here," he pointed to the remains of the ancient walls, now completely shrouded in darkness, "time flows so slowly that it approaches eternity. These stones absorb only a small part of the flow of time passing through the planet. They live and age for so long that they sometimes seem frozen."

He paused, seeing the confusion in Gilberto's eyes, and continued, "Eternity is a state in which there is no time. The past and future are replaced by one expanded present, encompassing all life. These places have not yet reached eternity, but they live in time so slowly that they consume much less of it than the rest of us. As time passes through them, the part they do not use settles on them in the form of stardust."

"Is this the stardust and the golden sparkles you collected in your bottle?" Gilberto guessed. "So you're collecting time itself here?"

"Exactly," Manuel nodded. "And thanks to it, we can at least somewhat maintain the normal flow of time on our planet. Of course, not for everyone," he added bitterly. "Your stardust will never be enough for the entire planet. But the grains of time we find here are enough to support the work of the scientific center where our scientists labor. We hope that sooner or later they will find the cause of our disrupted time and be able to correct it. This time is also sufficient to sustain the normal lives of the commandants."

"Who are the commandants?" Gilberto asked.

"They are the personal guard of our rulers," Manuel explained. "Their main task now is to oversee the collection of stardust and assist seekers like me in finding new places where it accumulates, untouched by people."

"Do you think people can somehow harm stardust?" Gilberto asked doubtfully.

"How else?" Manuel seemed annoyed by his lack of understanding. "With your speed of life, with your constant bustle, you automatically absorb all the time allotted to you. Just by being nearby, you draw every second of stardust into your frantic rhythm. You can burn everything around you and not even notice it!" Manuel's irritation was palpable.

"You say you cannot feel the present?" he continued angrily. "Believe me, if we were given the treasure you possess, we would savor it down to the very depth, to the slightest microsecond. We would absorb the joy of every moment as if it were the last of our lives. We would absorb its colors with all our souls and be happy to feel the joy of every breath of the breeze. We would gratefully accept everything that surrounds us and never forget how beautiful it is. For me, working on your planet is a real holiday, because only here can I now feel life in all its fullness."

"All this, of course, sounds good," Gilberto responded doubtfully. "But one can't just enjoy life and not think about the future at all."

"There is a big difference between the concepts of 'thinking about the future' and pointlessly pining about it," Manuel snapped. "You try to live in the future today, and this brings you nothing but unnecessary worries and illusions. You immerse yourself in the past as if it surrounds you right now, and instead of real sensations, you catch only their pathetic aftertaste, trying to change what cannot be changed. You have the opportunity to live here and now, but instead, you escape to a time that no longer exists or does not yet exist. How do you not understand that it is impossible to truly think about the future if you do not have the present? How can you make plans for your life if you don't know how to live? What tomorrow can you talk about if you don't have today? After all, any tomorrow, when it comes, will invariably become today."

Gilberto listened intently, trying to make out the ruins of the ancient Roman city in the darkness. If these walls were alive, they could probably tell a lot about how, before their eyes, era after era, generations of people were replaced, so different and at the same time so similar to each other. How petty and insignificant human suffering and fears must have seemed to them, stretching into one endless present. For a moment, Gilberto thought he saw this present—unified, all-encompassing, absorbing the past and the future. In this frozen moment, an inextricable connection of times was felt, and suddenly such a simple, but for some reason previously unknown, thought arose in Gilberto's mind: the future is impossible without the present.

"How strange everything turns out," he said thoughtfully. "In order to restore the passage of time, you need to get closer to eternity, that is, to a state in which there is no time."

"That's the difference between us," Manuel nodded. "You always have this opportunity, but you don't use it. You have the chance to cherish what you created yesterday and lay the foundation for your tomorrow, and yet you waste your life so mediocrely, squandering time, people, and relationships. If I had the time that you have, believe me, I would use it much better."

Gilberto was silent, trying to comprehend what he had heard. He tried to imagine a life without time, a strange existence in which all his previous works could be erased in an instant by the turn of an invisible wheel. Nothing durable or stable could simply survive in this bizarre temporal game. Relationships fell apart, plans collapsed, and even the present moment constantly slipped away, turning out to be a deception. He shuddered, imagining that in an instant he could lose everything dear to him. And then, as if in response to his fear, his consciousness was slashed by a sharp, arrow-like question: what exactly is dear to you?

Friends: Christian and Estherita! This realization struck him with the sharpness of lightning. His friends, the people he spent so much time with and who trusted him, were so easily destroyed by this time hunter!

"And what do you spend your life on?" he attacked Manuel. "Running like crazy around alien planets for gold dust that you can't even spend on yourself but have to give to these commandants? And for this reason, you kill people who are simply unlucky enough to get in your way?"

"I didn't kill anyone," Manuel snapped.

"Don't make an idiot out of me!" Gilberto shouted. "Those snakes that attacked my friends two days ago were your work! I don't believe that it could have happened without you."

"Yes, I did it," Manuel admitted coldly, an ominous smile playing on his lips. "I had to delay them and have time to collect the stardust before they erased it completely with their presence. But I told the snakes not to kill them, only to immobilize them. As soon as I finished my work, the snakes would let them go."

"So they are still alive?" Gilberto asked in a trembling voice. "Are you saying that they have been lying on the ground for more than two days, tied up, captured by snakes, while you are here filling a bottle with pollen?!" He choked with indignation. "We'll go to them right now, and you'll let them go!"

Manuel laughed. "You think you can force me to obey you?" he asked quietly through laughter. "I'm sorry I caused trouble for your friends, but they shouldn't have been wandering around. However, I was going to let them go anyway, just by teaching them a small lesson. Besides, now you came here and ruined my work anyway. So, perhaps, nothing prevents me now from visiting your friends and ridding them of the friendly company of snakes."

Gilberto remained silent in shame, realizing that this powerful guest from another planet was, in fact, unlikely to agree to carry out his orders. So he continued in a more peaceful, even pleading tone:

"I swear to you, if you free them, we will never go even a kilometer closer to the ancient ruins again."

Manuel laughed again and stepped deeper into the forest, motioning for Gilberto to follow him.

* * *

Snakes slithered over their skin in ominous, wavy ribbons, creating the deceptive illusion that they might soon slip off them and disappear into the ground from which they had so unexpectedly appeared. Yet, no such miracle transpired, and the steel grip of their elastic bodies did not weaken for a moment. The second night was approaching, and hope was melting before their eyes, dissolving almost entirely. A painful death awaited them, and the snakes seemed intent on prolonging their agony without inflicting visible harm to their victims.

Occasionally, the serpents allowed Christian and Estherita to move, and they would sit down with relief, pressing their backs against the tree trunk, unable to believe the nightmare was over. This disbelief was justified: as soon as one of them hoped to rise, the snakes would arch in warning and rush at them again. A few times, they allowed the prisoners to reach the food supplies, silently observing with narrowed eyes as they hastily consumed the remnants of their provisions.

More than once they'd tried to speak with their implacable guards, but it was futile—the snakes continued to diligently watch over them, as if executing some cruel and senseless order. Desperate to escape their tight rings, Christian gazed helplessly at the twilight creeping down from the mountains and painfully realized that, in his unexpectedly short life, he had never truly known happiness.

The thirst for happiness, intensified by the premonition of inexorable death, now burned through him like a red-hot iron from within. Blood pulsated, accelerating through his veins, but they, swelling, pressed against the wall of cold snake scales.

"I love you," Christian said calmly, looking into the darkening sky. It was very simple, simpler than anything else. Nothing ambiguous or complex remained in his mind. The simplicity and integrity of the moment that gripped him was absolute, and within it was only one truth, one feeling that truly mattered—his love for Estherita.

"I know, honey," she responded. "I love you too."

"No, you don't know!" Christian objected with unexpected fervor. "You can't know this, because until recently I didn't know it myself. Your father was right, I was never worthy of you."

"Don't say that," Estherita began, but Christian abruptly interrupted her. He tensed, instinctively standing up, and the snakes, with the precision of a flawless mechanism, tightened their grip on his arms and legs. He didn't care. Christian felt ready to rush into mortal combat with the serpents that had entangled him, unafraid of suffocating in their steel embrace or dying from deadly poison.

"I'm telling the truth," he said sharply. "Even when we started dating, I didn't know... I didn't know that I would love you," he forced out with effort. "And your father did not lie about me being a thief. I was in a gang that robbed travelers on the roads, and I had no equal in raiding houses. If I were him, I would simply shoot such a boyfriend of my daughter. Digging up Roman graves seems like child's play compared to my other adventures. But with all this, I want you to know that I do truly love you, Estherita, and that you are dearer to me than anything in the world."

She was silent, and the silence that surrounded them became even more ominous. Pain, disappointment, disbelief—all these feelings rose in waves in her soul, and even the snakes seemed to sympathetically loosen their grip, sensing her confusion.

Christian took a deep breath of the cool evening air, feeling that every moment could be their last. His whole life unfolded before him in all its clarity and completeness, like one grand picture, and the feeling of total meaninglessness fell upon him, heavier than the weight of the snakes. How much suffering had he brought to people, trying to take possession of others' belongings, and for what? Could anything he stole save him now?

"Forgive me," he said with feeling, trying to turn to Estherita. "I can't die knowing that you haven't forgiven me. I brought you into this, and I know that all of this happened because of me. If I could fix anything, I swear I would change my whole life. I would cherish this happiness like the apple of my eye, and would never, for any treasure, agree to part with you. I couldn't tell you the truth at first, and then I didn't tell it because I was afraid of losing you. More than anything in the world, I'm afraid of losing you."

"I love you, and you know it," she answered quietly.

The night enveloped them more and more, and Christian felt that this would be their last night. Suddenly he heard a rustling in the bushes—wild animals must have already rushed here, hoping to feast on easy prey.

"Christian, Estherita, it's me, Gilberto!" they heard a familiar voice. At that moment, as if on cue, the snakes' grip began to weaken. Another second—and their jailers slid into the grass in nimble zigzags, disappearing without a trace. Gilberto emerged from the bushes, and next to him stood another short man in a ridiculous gold suit. A strange golden glow emanated from his face. Still not believing in his salvation, Christian began to get up—at first hesitantly, and then, gradually getting used to the joy of movement, he rushed headlong towards Estherita.

"Stop!" the golden man suddenly ordered him. Not understanding anything, Christian froze in his tracks and stared at the stranger, who, to his amazement, knelt before him and pulled out a strange vessel from his bosom. He opened its lid and froze, and then before the eyes of the astonished Christian, a stream of golden pollen stretched from the ground, settling directly into the bottle.

"How did you do that?" the stranger asked in surprise, looking up at Christian.

"What do you mean?" Christian replied.

"Stardust!" the little man exclaimed. "This is the first time that I've ever seen stardust next to people."

"Stardust is time," Gilberto hastily explained. "If it appeared, it means that time seemed to stop for you for a moment, as if you had been somewhere where there is no time."

"No time?" Christian asked, uncomprehending. "But time passed, and day gave way to night, albeit very slowly. By the change of day and night, I realized that two days had already passed, and these were the most terrible days of my life. I understood and rethought a lot during these days, but I did nothing except think about my life, what it had been, and whether it had any meaning."

"Apparently, in the life of every person there are moments when he comes into contact with eternity, which means that he falls out of the flow of time," Manuel suggested. "At such moments, time settles around him like stardust. It is strange that the commandants did not notice this feature. Because now, if we start looking for stardust around people, we can surely collect enough of it to restore the passage of time on our planet."

"But maybe the commandants don't really want this?" Gilberto suddenly suggested. "Who knows, maybe they are quite happy with the fact that only they could live a normal life, giving them enormous power, compared to the others. If I were you, when you collect enough stardust, I would not share it with the commandants, but try to transfer it directly to people or at least scientists. Your problem might be solved much faster."

Manuel looked at him incredulously, then nodded, hiding the bottle in his bosom.

"Thank you for trying to help my planet. Perhaps there is truth in your words, and it can change our lives."

"You also changed our lives," Gilberto responded sincerely. "Thank you so much. I don't know what will happen next, but we will never forget your lesson."

The golden man smiled, suddenly rose above the ground, and disappeared into the air, as if he himself were made of mysterious stardust. The three friends silently watched him vanish, their gaze lingering on the stars shedding their light on the ruins of the ancient Roman city.

A Tale of Brave Dwarves

AFTER THE STORM, THE FOREST breathed pure, untouched air—the kind that emerges only after nature has been washed clean. The fragrance of wet earth mingled with the scent of herbs, creating an intoxicating aroma that wrapped itself around her as if embracing her with its whole being. Each leaf and blade of grass shimmered, laden with droplets of rain that clung to them as though reluctant to let go. In the sunlight, those droplets became jewels, catching the light and transforming into tiny flames. The sun, breaking through the canopy above, danced in the treetops like a cascade of lanterns, each flicker a playful reflection of light and shadow. Every living thing seemed to drink in the sun's warmth and could not take in enough, as if the forest itself was bursting into bloom, filled with vital juices. The trees stretched their branches upward, yearning for the sky, while the earth below responded with a vibrant, colorful mosaic.

Nicole stood amidst it all, smiling softly as she watched the elves—tiny and delicate—darting among the flower petals, their wings glistening in the sunlight. The flower elves, radiant in their joy, twirled among the rain elves, and the air hummed with the sound of their wings. The forest, once hushed in anticipation, had now sprung back to life. Large butterflies swooped towards the blossoms, their sudden movement sending the elves scattering. Birds began to sing with full-throated abandon, eager to announce the storm's end to the world. Beetles crawled along the polished, rain-slicked leaves, and every now and then, a flash of hare ears could be seen peeking from behind the bushes.

Everything here was familiar, intimately so. Nicole felt an unspoken connection with every leaf, every flower, every blade of grass. It was as though the forest recognized her, picked her up in its arms, and carried her, drowning her in its diversity and giving her a feeling of infinity. The very essence of the woods enveloped her, and she was carried away by its endless beauty, lost in the sense of boundless joy. The forest was alive, woven from the very matter from which all living things were once born. This matter, thin as the threads of a web, bound everything together, creating a space that was in-finite and continuous.

Nicole felt this on a deep, almost sacred level. With each passing moment, she realized how incredibly fortunate she was to call this enchanted place her home. The mere thought of leaving it, of being torn from this paradise, stabbed at her heart. The image of a big city filled her with dread, with its looming specter of loneliness and the cold, indifferent streets. As though summoned by her thoughts, Daniel appeared, emerging from behind a bush.

Nicole rushed to him in some kind of desperate joy, as though every meeting might be their last.

"Have your parents changed their minds?" he asked, his voice filled with hope.

Nicole shook her head, her eyes brimming with tears. "No," she answered, her voice trembling. "Father is as stubborn as ever, and Mother... she always agrees with him. If it weren't for those rumors Aunt Molly picked up, everything would be fine."

"What exactly is Aunt Molly saying?" Daniel pressed, as if clinging to the hope that there was some loophole which could reverse her parents' decision.

"She says the king has granted our forest to some power-ful duke. And this duke apparently plans to clear our part of the woods to build a grand castle, with sprawling pastures and farmlands. So Father thinks it's best we leave before it's too late, " Nicole explained, her voice bitter.

"And don't forget," she added, her frustration bubbling up, "he used to be a brownie. He lived in a home with humans for years, and he's always missed that life. Ever since Aunt Molly married Uncle Julien and they came into possession of that estate, Father's been obsessed. Not a day goes by that he doesn't talk about how our relatives now have a grand estate with room for dozens of brownies. I think," Nicole said, her voice heavy with sorrow, "that this news about the duke was exactly what he needed to justify his decision."

"Have you ever seen this estate?" Daniel asked, his brow furrowed with curiosity.

"Once—at Aunt Molly's wedding," Nicole replied, her voice tinged with frustration. "Believe me, it's nothing special. A ruin, really. Sure, there are some impressive spots here and there, but it's lifeless—dull beyond words. The only thing growing is grass, pushing up through the cracks in the floors. There's nothing else, nothing alive!" Her words trailed off in despair. "It's just a pile of crumbling walls, dying brick by brick. I don't understand why Dad finds the forest that bad."

"If it's all about the duke's plans, then surely we could move deeper into the forest," Daniel suggested, his voice carrying a glimmer of hope. "He can't cut down the whole forest, can he?"

"I already tried that argument," Nicole said, her tone heavy with resignation. "But Dad insists there's no way to predict how far the logging will go. He doesn't want to live in constant fear that our home might be destroyed at any moment. He's convinced that the estate offers stability—a fresh start. He keeps telling us we'll love it, that it's the only sensible choice."

"But what if the rumors about the duke are just that—rumors?" Daniel pressed, clinging to the faint hope. "What if nothing's going to happen?"

"Of course, that's possible," Nicole shot back, her voice edged with frustration. "But we have no proof. And neither does Aunt Molly! The only difference is that Dad believes what he wants to believe."

"I can't believe you're leaving," Daniel said quietly.

"Neither can I," Nicole murmured, her eyes filling with tears. The sun caught them, turning each drop into its tiny reflection as it had previously reflected in the pearls of dew scattered throughout the forest. The scents of the woods seemed to embrace her even tighter, as though the forest was reluctant to let her go, weaving its intoxicating aromas around her.

Without thinking, Daniel pulled her into a hug. His voice took on a sudden, reckless determination. "What if we go to the city and find this duke ourselves? If we can learn what he's really planning, maybe it'll help your parents make a sensible decision. Worst case, Aunt Molly's right, and we'll all lose our homes. But for now, there's still a small chance it's all just gossip."

Nicole looked at him with doubt, but deep within her, a flicker of hope began to stir. The uncertainty was unbearable, gnawing at her day and night. And Daniel's idea—however impulsive—didn't seem so reckless after all. The desire to know the truth was growing stronger by the minute.

"Aunt Molly did say the duke lives in a grand, sumptuous castle," Nicole mused aloud, the beginnings of a plan forming in her mind. "But castles have brownies, too. We could find his brownie, explain our situation, and maybe he'll let us in. I'm sure he'd help us hear firsthand what the duke is planning. We, gnomes, are the closest relatives of brownies. We're bound to help each other, right?" She paused, her resolve wavering for a moment. "But the journey to the city is long. Our parents will go mad when they realize we've disappeared."

"Just think how happy they'll be if we bring back good news," Daniel said, his eyes shining with conviction. "We're not taking any real risks. We'll just go, listen to what's happening, and come back with the truth."

Nicole's hesitation slowly melted away. "Yes," she nodded, her voice steady now. "In this situation, I think we have no choice." The thought of a long journey frightened her, but at the same time, her belief in their mission grew stronger. They weren't doing this just for themselves—they were doing it for the forest, their beloved home, so full of life and warmth. They had to uncover the truth, and they would do it!

* * *

The city welcomed the gnomes with sprawling, haphazard streets, sloppily dotted by uneven clusters of houses. As they ventured deeper toward the heart of the city, the streets narrowed, their stone walls closing in like a tightening grip. Even the air, pressed into these cramped spaces, seemed to suffocate under the weight of them.

"How can anyone live in these tunnels?" Nicole exclaimed, her voice sharp with disbelief.

The stone labyrinth ensnared them, its twisting passages offering a false promise of escape only to pull them deeper into its stony web. It encircled them, replacing the open earth and sky with looming, heavy walls that hung above like jagged cliffs. The city itself seemed alive, a predatory force that swallowed them whole, dragging them into its depths. And then, as though it could no longer bear the strain of its own pressure, it spat them out into the open expanse of a square. Before them loomed towering Gothic cathedrals, massive and imposing as if they sought to make the heavens tremble with awe at the sight of their grandeur.

The duke's castle stood distant from the bustle, a small city unto itself. Between the various buildings of the estate ran streets of their own—yet unlike those in the city, these were wide, welcoming. They did not crush or crowd; instead, they beckoned, drawing in the uninvited with the allure of architectural beauty and the promise of safety in their solid, towering walls. The walls, so thick and monolithic, seemed capable of swallowing a person whole, consuming him in their silent strength. The streets unfurled in pristine order, as clean and precise as palace corridors.

In the castle's inner courtyard, trees defiantly grew between the stones, and beside them lay a carefully tended garden. Bathed in the light spilling from the windows, the branches seemed to glow, as though striving to become lanterns themselves, eager to merge with the intricate man-made world around them. This world descended upon the gnomes in all its might—its grandeur and latent power—and though it was breathtaking in its beauty, it felt devoid of life. Daniel and Nicole felt diminished by its magnificence, unsettled by the cold splendor.

An ancient brownie greeted them within the duke's castle. The gnomes were taken aback by his solitude in such a huge space, for he was the only one who lived here—there were no bustling children, no noisy grandchildren to fill the halls with life. After listening to their plea, the brownie shrugged, his expression tinged with doubt.

"I hate to dash your hopes," he said with a sigh, "but I doubt much good will come of this. You're aiming to pierce the heart of malice, deceit, and endless intrigue. How can you be sure that even by eavesdropping on his conversations, you'll learn the truth? People are fickle and treacherous—they change their minds on a whim, lie even to those they love most. I've lived here for many long years, and I've seen more evil, betrayal, and hollow dreams—things people, for some reason, call their plans—than I can count. I've forgotten how to trust words. Many brownies once lived here, but they couldn't withstand the poison of constant intrigue. The more powerful and wealthy the master, the less life remains in his house." He finished with a somber nod.

"Still, we must try," Daniel insisted, unwavering. "The future of our home, of everything we hold dear, depends on it."

"Try, then," the brownie shrugged once more. "Perhaps fortune will favor you, and you'll find what you're searching for."

Buoyed by his reluctant blessing, Daniel and Nicole ventured into the castle's grandest building. Its corridors mirrored the streets they had passed outside—smooth, flawless, framed by walls like jewels set in an ornate frame. The rooms exuded opulence and that rare sense of perfection that arises from the fusion of extreme wealth and impeccable taste.

That very evening, the duke sat in his study, its furnishings austere but elegant, conversing in low tones with his trusted aide. The gnomes crept to the door, scarcely daring to breathe as they strained to catch every word.

"It is imperative that this report not be dispatched under my name," the duke murmured, his voice barely audible, as though he feared even the walls of his own abode might overhear. "Thus, the King will be persuaded that I am not the sole bearer of this opinion."

"The most vital task is to ensure the truth never reaches him," responded a second voice, equally subdued.

The duke chuckled softly. "There is no danger of that. His Majesty has long surrounded himself with sycophants who tell him only what he wishes to hear. The King is foolish and vain; he believes what he likes to believe. He underestimates the strength and power of his enemy, and places too much trust in the aid of his allies. But when he entangles himself in war, when the entire nation is engulfed by hunger, and when lines of coffins flow through the streets, the people will come to despise their ruler, and I will be in a position to depose him with ease."

Daniel and Nicole froze, exchanging silent glances. What they had overheard did not pertain to the forest, yet it was no less significant—perhaps even more so. The treacherous duke aspired to drag the kingdom into war to usurp power! Was he prepared to spill rivers of blood, filling the streets of this labyrinthine city? Nicole shuddered as she envisioned the city, overwhelmed by pain and hatred, exploding with the force of the bloodshed. If even the air felt confined within its stone tunnels, how could such a seething, molten feeling be contained?

"Are people truly capable of destroying not only the lives of others but also their own, all for the sake of power?" Nicole whispered to Daniel. "The life of their city, their country?" She struggled to imagine any forest dweller daring to plunge their sunlit homeland into such a bloody abyss; her mind recoiled at the thought.

"This is monstrous!" Daniel exclaimed softly. "We must find a way to warn the King."

"And how do you propose to do that?" the old brownie asked after listening to their confused account. "Humans cannot see or hear gnomes, just as they are deaf to us, brownies. They often fail to listen even to their own kind, let alone creatures like us. We can only establish contact with children by entering their dreams, a nd even then, only because the dream fairies have some influence over children's sleep. Adults' dreams, being composed of fragments of their memories, secret desires, and fears, are beyond our reach."

"Then we must find a child and convey our information through a dream," Nicole said decisively. "Are there any children in this castle?"

"The duke has no children," the brownie replied curtly. "The only child that comes to mind is the son of one of the cooks. His nanny quit a few years ago, and it seems that their poor, large family could not afford a new one. So, when the youngest son grew a little older, his mother began to bring him to work. He spends his time in the kitchen, forbidden to leave, for the duke detests children's laughter. But this child does not sleep here; he sleeps at home. If you wish to enter his dreams, you must first go to his home and negotiate with the brownies there."

"We will negotiate," Daniel assured him. "Just tell me where this boy lives."

Leaving the duke's castle, the gnomes hurried to the address provided by their new acquaintance. The city enveloped them once more, drawing them into its labyrinths while simultaneously trying to push them out. It now seemed hidden, frozen in a tense, gloomy anticipation of impending destruction. Though still peaceful, it appeared to hope to forever imprint itself on reality in this state: majestic and unscathed.

The streetlights finally illuminated the streets, shining like flawless scenery. However, over time, this flawlessness diminished. The roads, once smooth like parquet, gave way to cobblestones, increasingly uneven and protruding from the ground. The stone walls, though still noble, were now accompanied by growing filth, which at first seemed blasphemous but gradually became a natural part of the city's intricate fabric. From a world of beauty and wealth, the gnomes had entered a realm of neediness, if not outright poverty.

After much searching, they finally found the right house—modest, yet quite tidy. Along with the human occupants, a charming couple of brownies resided there: Martin and Adele. When the gnomes relayed their tale, Adele sighed heavily and began, with cautious words:

"I understand that what you've learned feels momentous, that it seems like a matter of life and death. And you're probably right, but you have no idea of the world you've stumbled upon. It's a world ruled by cruelty and treachery, where notions of good and evil hold no meaning."

"But in this case, it's simple," Daniel replied, bewildered. "The duke is scheming not only against his country but also his King. If the ruler discovers one of his subjects aims to overthrow him, he will quickly deal with the traitor and reward whoever brought him the truth."

"If only it were that simple, my dear boy." Adele gave a sad, knowing smile. "Years ago, I met a ghost. He lived in the very estate where your Aunt Molly and Uncle Julien now reside," she said, nodding toward Nicole.

"When that ghost was a human, serving in the royal guard, he uncovered that one of the high-ranking nobles was a traitor and embezzler," Adele continued. "He, too, believed the world would rise in righteous fury once the truth came to light. Young and headstrong, he thought his truth was so obvious, so undeniable, that victory was inevitable. But the truth, as he learned too late, mattered to no one. The nobleman was so powerful that he crushed the naive guardsman without effort. The incident ruined a good man's life and nearly cost him eternity. And that was an adult. Now you want to involve a child in this dangerous affair!"

Nicole, troubled by Adele's words but unwilling to back down, muttered, "But if we succeed, we might save the lives of thousands of children. This duke threatens not just our home, but yours as well. We have to try. Yes, he's only a child, but that's why he'll likely escape punishment, even if no one believes him."

"I can't forbid you from talking to the fairy of dreams," Adele sighed. "But I fear you're too pure for the filth you're about to wade into. Innocent beings can't win in the dirty games of this world, no matter how noble their intentions. Worse yet, this filth has a way of staining even the purest souls, disfiguring them beyond recognition."

* * *

The conversation with the fairy of dreams was no easier than any they had faced so far. After hearing the gnomes out, she gazed at them with doubt in her eyes and spoke sternly:

"How do you imagine this will work? You're asking me to let the taint of adult deceit and intrigue seep into the purity of children's dreams. I don't even know how such darkness could be woven into the delicate fabric of their dreams."

"But real war is far worse than a troubling dream!" Daniel protested passionately. "If a single difficult dream could save many children from real suffering, don't you think it's worth the risk?"

"And even if I manage it," the fairy continued, her voice sharp, "do you realize the danger you're placing this child in? Whoever he tells about his dream, it could ruin him."

"What if we ask the child, in the dream, to write a note when he wakes up?" Nicole suggested, suddenly struck by an idea. "We could find a way to slip the note to the King ourselves, and no one would ever know where it came from. We would write it ourselves, if only we knew how."

"Dismiss that thought," the fairy said curtly. "Even if you could write, you're forbidden from exchanging correspondence with humans. The oldest laws of the universe decree that brownies and gnomes must remain unseen by people. Direct interaction with them would violate all those laws." She paused, considering for a moment. "But... if we merely ask the child to write a note describing what he saw in his dream and leave it somewhere, I believe we can allow such a small breach. The situation is dire enough to justify this much interference." She nodded gravely. "I will try to help you."

Daniel and Nicole could not fathom what exactly the cook's son had witnessed in his dream, but the following day, after departing from the warm hospitable house of Martin and Adele, they once again hastened toward the duke's castle. Morning bathed the city in light, transforming it into a far more vibrant and joyous place than the night before. The sun poured itself generously over the streets, and its rays penetrated even the narrowest alleys, seeking to fill them with healing light. Sliding between the cracks in the stone, darting along the jagged edges of shadows, the sunlight seemed to mend the very soul of the city, infusing it with renewed hope.

Life shimmered softly in every street corner, every diminutive courtyard, every tent where vendors hawked their wares. The gnomes could feel the city's breath, a desperate and nearly pleading pulse that reached out to them. If, the day before, the city had seemed lifeless, today Daniel and Nicole felt its energy surging, alive and vibrant, much like the wilds of their native forest. Though they had not yet learned to commune with the city as they did with the forest—where they could sense its smallest breath—they had begun to respond to its call. And they knew, instinctively, that they had to help.

The old brownie who guarded the castle greeted them with even more skepticism than the day prior, but this time, without a word, he allowed them to pass. The gnomes hurried toward the kitchen, their movements swift and eager, despite the brownie's muttered complaint as they scurried by:

"Blasted noisy creatures, echoing through these halls. Have they no sense of how to dwell alongside humans?"

In the duke's kitchen, the clamor of preparation filled the air. Multiple dishes simmered on the stove, the heat from it radiating through the room. Cooks worked diligently at the long tables, chopping vegetables, slicing meat, their hands moving with the rhythm of practiced ease. In the corner, a small boy sat hunched over, writing something intently on a scrap of paper.

"Let me see what you've got there," his mother said softly, bending down to take the paper from him. As her eyes scanned the page, her expression shifted, darkening with sudden alarm. She stepped back, horror flashing across her face, and she pounced on the child.

"Never—do you hear me? Never write down such dreams again!" she commanded, her tone filled with genuine fear. "I don't know how you could dream such a thing, but you must banish it from your mind. And you must never tell a soul about it."

"But I can't forget it," the boy protested, his small voice steady with conviction. "The fairy who came to me in the dream said I must write it down—to save the city."

"You will not save this city, and no one else will, either!" his mother snapped, her face hardening. "If you continue with this, you will ruin us all. How dare you write such things about the duke, especially in his own house?" Her words were filled with outrage.

The boy lowered his gaze but said nothing more. The gnomes, who had been silently observing this scene, exchanged troubled glances. Finally, Nicole, her voice barely above a whisper, spoke up:

"My dear, could you write just one more note? Just one. After that, leave it to us. You won't need to involve yourself any further."

The boy glanced around as though he could hear them, but the meaning of their words escaped him. He waited until his mother turned her back, and for the first time since they had arrived in the duke's palace, he slipped out of the kitchen and dashed down the corridor.

"Oh no!" Daniel groaned, his voice laden with dread. "He's gone to tell everything himself!"

Unable to suppress their mounting anxiety, Daniel and Nicole darted after the child. The boy burst out into the palace garden, where immaculate flower beds bloomed in perfect symmetry, majestic trees stretched their branches overhead, and bushes trimmed to geometric precision lined the paths. An old gardener worked amidst this display of nature's discipline, bent over, carefully mowing the grass, ensuring that not a single leaf dared disrupt the spherical shape of the low trees. He straightened slowly, blinking in surprise at the boy.

"Where did you come from, little one?" he asked warily, his eyes narrowing. "What are you doing here?"

"I need to tell you something very important," the boy began, his voice faltering as he tried to catch his breath. "We must find a way to get a message to the King—something vital."

"To the King?" The gardener chuckled, though unease flickered in his eyes. "And what would you be telling his majesty, eh?"

"I know for a fact," the boy blurted out, his words tumbling over one another, "that the duke is planning to deceive him, to lead him into war. He's lying—he's saying it'll be easy to win, but it won't. He wants the King's men to tire and grow angry, so he can overthrow him and take the crown!"

The gardener's expression shifted from amusement to horror. He recoiled, glancing nervously over his shoulder. "What on earth are you talking about, boy? Do you have any idea what could happen to us for such a talk? Where did you even hear this?"

"They told me..." the boy trailed off, his gaze dropping to the ground. He obviously realized that mentioning a fairy and a dream in such a situation was not the right thing to do.

"Who told you?" the gardener pressed, anxiety creeping into his voice. "Who would say such a thing to a child, especially in the duke's castle? id you overhear the duke's conversation yourself?"

The boy remained stubbornly silent, his eyes fixed on the dirt at his feet.

"Even if—" the gardener hesitated, rubbing his weathered hands. "Even if you did hear something, and understood it correctly, and even if—heaven forbid—it were all true... this is a matter far beyond a child's concern. And beyond mine too! I won't be the one to deliver such news."

"Why not?" the boy cried, his face burning with indignation. "This information could save us all!"

"Because," the gardener replied, his voice sharp with fear, "the King's wrath is more likely to fall on the bearer of bad news than on the one who plots against him. I'll not become a victim of royal anger. What does it matter to me, anyway, if war comes? I'm old, I won't be called to fight. The duke's castle walls are thick; whatever happens beyond them, we'll be safe here. We can't change anything, and the only thing I can do is protect myself."

"But those who are not behind these walls—those who are out there—they'll die!" the boy cried, his voice breaking with desperation.

"Quiet!" the gardener hissed, glancing around in terror. "First of all, all this could be some wild fantasy of yours. I'll not risk my life for that. Secondly, as I've already told you, nothing we do will change the course of events. It's better to mind our own business and stay out of affairs that don't concern us."

"Cowardice," Daniel muttered in disgust as he watched from the shadows. "How selfish these humans can be. They think only of themselves, blind to the fact that shared suffering will soon find its way to them as well."

The boy, his eyes blazing with frustration, seemed just as outraged as the gnomes. Still clinging to a fragile hope of finding someone willing to listen, he bolted from the garden and out onto the palace's main street, heading straight for the gates. A guard stood there, resplendent in a gilded uniform, his hand resting on the pommel of his sword. He looked down at the boy with cold, detached curiosity as if he couldn't quite believe the small figure before him was even human.

"Are you a soldier?" the boy asked, a glimmer of hope flickering in his eyes as he gazed up at the towering guard.

"I guard this castle," the man replied, his voice thick with pride. "But tell me, why are you running around here alone, unsupervised?"

The boy's face crumpled, his voice trembling as he spoke. "I'm trying to find someone who can deliver a message to the King. It's important—it could save the entire country!"

The guard let out a harsh laugh, his amusement cruel and condescending. "Save the country? You?" He shook his head. "Listen, kid, saving a country is the work of professionals."

"The duke is planning a war!" The boy's words burst forth with a desperate resolve, though his gaze faltered, sliding to the ground.

The guard's smile faded instantly. The word duke seemed to trigger something deep and severe in him. His expression tightened, and a shadow crossed his face.

"The duke? Impossible." The guard frowned, his voice turning cold. "The duke doesn't plan wars. Wars are a royal concern, but even the King never plans anything like that. Only our enemies plot such things. Understand this for the rest of your life."

"But the duke wants the King to start this war!" the boy insisted, confused by his words. "He knows it will be difficult war—impossible even—and he hopes it will weaken the King so he can overthrow him."

The guard's face hardened, and his hand moved instinctively to his sword. "So, that's what you say about our duke?" he barked, his voice sharp with menace.

"But it's the truth!" the boy cried, his words defiant even as fear crept into his voice.

"I don't care if it's true or not!" the guard snapped, his grip tightening around the boy's shoulder. "The duke must know about the slander you're spreading in his castle!"

"But we must stop the war!" the boy pleaded, struggling against the guard's iron grip. "If it starts, you'll be sent to the front—and you might die!"

"Stopping wars isn't my duty," the guard said flatly, his voice unyielding. "My duty is to protect the duke and report anything suspicious. You'll tell him yourself where you got these vile rumors."

Nicole, watching helplessly, gasped. "Anything but that! Adele was right—we've dragged this child into something far worse than we imagined."

Without a word, the gnomes rushed after the guard as he dragged the struggling boy toward the massive entrance of the palace. Daniel spotted a loose stone near the wall and hurled it with all his might at the guard's feet. The guard stumbled, clumsily trying to maintain his balance. In the confusion, his grip loosened, and the boy wrenched himself free, bolting down the echoing corridors, his small footsteps fading into the distance.

The guard, unable to stay on his feet, collapsed awkwardly onto the cold stone floor just outside the heavy wooden doors. His furious voice echoed after the boy: "I'll find you again, you little brat! And when I do, you'll regret it!"

Daniel and Nicole stood frozen, amazed and crushed by the scene they had witnessed. Slowly, they turned back toward the castle.

"I don't understand these people at all," Nicole confessed, confused. "In our forest, if someone discovered a danger threatening everyone, he would warn the entire forest. He'd be a hero. But this soldier—he follows orders blindly, without even realizing that he's betraying the country he's sworn to protect. He might even die because of this war without any sense. How can anyone act like that?"

"I warned you not to meddle in people's affairs," came the raspy voice of the old brownie. "You're too pure, too untouched by the world's grime. You believe that your kind of logic governs everything. But these creatures live by rules we cannot grasp, and never will."

Nicole, her voice heavy with despair, asked, "So what do we do now?"

"Perhaps," Daniel ventured uncertainly, "we could seek out the duke again, listen to his schemes one last time."

"But why?" Nicole's voice was drained of color. "What point is there in torturing ourselves further if we already know we are powerless to change anything?"

Daniel sighed, his breath tinged with resignation. "I don't know. Maybe it's the last thread we cling to, to quiet our conscience. One last effort to learn something before we leave here forever."

They sought the duke again, finding him in his study with his ever-loyal adjutant. His face radiated an unnatural enthusiasm, like a man on the brink of a triumph only he could see.

"Everything is proceeding as planned," he declared, the conviction in his voice more for himself than anyone else. "Yes, it has taken longer than anticipated, and required more effort, but now I have no doubt. The King received my last report, and that was the crucial part. Of course, it was naive to think a single document would convince him, but as they say, constant pressure wears away the hardest stone. Tomorrow, at dawn, His Majesty and I will hunt in the forest he gifted me. There, I'll secure his final decision to start the war. The King will feel that all his courtiers, without having conspired, are advising the same course. He'll be unable to doubt its wisdom. By tomorrow, our goal will be within reach."

"This is outrageous!" Nicole gasped. "He not only planned this—he chose our forest as the stage for his vile plot!"

"Wait," Daniel interrupted her. "This could be our last chance. Remember what you said: if one of our kind learned of such danger, he would rush to warn every living soul in the forest. Perhaps Adele and the brownie were right—we shouldn't try to fight evil on its own terms. The laws that govern its domain are beyond us. But now, the evil has encroached upon our land. And there, we may stand a chance."

"But how will we warn the others?" Nicole's gaze darted around the room, searching for some unseen ally. "We can't return home before dusk, and by nightfall, all the creatures will be asleep. By dawn, it will be too late."

"Perhaps there's someone who can reach the forest before we do," Daniel replied, refusing to give up. "Surely, in this concrete labyrinth, there must be something alive besides people."

"Why not seek Martin and Adele's counsel?" Nicole suggested. "They've lived here their entire lives; they must know who to turn to in such a dire moment."

They hurried back to the city, but this time its streets no longer felt sinister or threatening. The city had become familiar, even mundane. It spread itself before them, its streets stretching and curling like slow rivers. Wide avenues hummed with the distant murmur of market stalls and the steady pulse of the city's own life, understandable only to it. The path to the hospitable brownies' home was well-worn now, and the gnomes hurried along it, indistinguishable from the people in their hurry.

Adele listened intently to their plea, her brow furrowed in thought. Then she nodded, a glint of encouragement in her eyes. "This time, I believe you are right. Now, you fight within the bounds of your power. When good tries to battle evil on its own terms, it either dies or becomes too much like its enemy. It is far wiser to find support among your kind and face the threat together. I think I know who can help you."

Adele's voice softened as she continued, "There's a flower elf who lives near your aunt and uncle's estate, Nicole. He once proved an excellent messenger—he delivered his task with perfect precision. I trust he will not fail you now."

Together, they ventured to the old, abandoned manor on the city's outskirts. Time had left its scars on the grand estate, yet it stood tall, still majestic, towering over the neat, newer homes surrounding it like a somber monument to bygone days and their tragedies.

"Where are you, little elf?" Adele's voice was soft but firm as it echoed through the stillness. "You aided us greatly once before, and we are in need of your help once more."

Daniel and Nicole stood tense, their breath caught in the quiet, straining to hear any sign of life in the thick silence. The moments dragged on, heavy with uncertainty. But then, cutting through the still air, came the faint, delicate ringing of elven wings.

* * *

The forest at dawn shimmered with the soft radiance of early light, each beam awakening a vivid palette of colors. The long-awaited rays of the sun had pierced through, but the woods had yet to fully sate themselves, absorbing the light with the greed of all things ripening. It had not yet succumbed to the lethargy of midday heat; rather, it was just coming alive, drawing deep from the rich essence of the approaching day. Broad chestnuts cast generous shades across the earth, while towering firs, with their long, needle-like branches, spread their majestic branches.

From their lofty heights, it seemed as though blue-green waves cascaded down, like invisible streams flowing from mountaintops, their crests rippling with the breeze. Slender aspens swayed flirtatiously in time with the firs, their delicate branches bending in rhythm. When the wind grew bolder, it felt as though tongues of green flame flickered and intertwined, merging into one eternal, graceful dance. Fire, water, earth, and air—here, in this dawn-lit forest, all the elements of the world seemed to unite in a seamless celebration of life.

But the duke felt none of this. To him, the forest was no more alive than the green paint on the walls in one of the rooms of his castle. His mind was preoccupied, watching the King with cautious, sidelong glances, trying to gauge his mood. Suddenly, the duke noticed a strange, greenish mist creeping from the bushes, like vapor rising from a swamp. He glanced at the King again, but His Majesty seemed utterly unaware, riding his horse in a state of serene cheerfulness.

"What is that, Your Majesty?" the duke asked, his voice tight with unease as he watched the mist snake closer, its tendrils slowly winding around him.

"What do you mean?" replied the King, his tone light. "It's a splendid day, though we've yet to see any game."

The duke cast a worried look at the guards riding behind them, but they, too, appeared oblivious to the strange fog. Only his horse seemed to sense the danger, growing increasingly restless. The steed stumbled, snorting anxiously, before freezing in place, its gaze fixed on something within the thicket. The duke, following its line of sight, turned—and froze. A pair of luminous blue eyes stared back at him, belonging to a snow-white unicorn. The creature's gaze was piercing, its otherworldly beauty both mesmerizing and terrifying. It lowered its head ever so slightly, and the tip of its gleaming horn pointed at the duke like an arrow poised on a bowstring.

In that moment, the duke realized the unicorn was somehow communicating with his horse. The steed's ears twitched, attuned to a silent message only it could understand. Then, without warning, the horse moved, stepping deliberately into the thicket.

"Stop, you stupid beast!" the duke shouted, yanking on the reins. But the horse only accelerated, crashing through branches that lashed at the duke's face like whips. The more he fought to control it, the faster the horse ran, until the King and his retinue faded from view. The forest grew denser, darker, as if closing in around him. His heart pounded with panic as the horse, tired of the constant tugging at the reins, suddenly reared up and, with cold indifference, threw the duke to the ground. He hit the earth hard, dazed, as the towering trees loomed over him, and the green mist swirled menacingly in the air.

The duke staggered to his feet, glancing around with unease. The forest, which moments before had seemed so inviting, as if it would welcome any traveler into its green embrace, now bristled with hostility, like a fortress poised for battle. Then, as if summoned by his very thoughts, an actual wall materialized among the trees. It looked eerily similar to the battlements of his own castle, and the duke stood there, bewildered, unable to fathom how such a structure could have appeared in the heart of the forest.

Suddenly, a sharp whistle split the air—loud as a cannon blast, sharp as an arrow's flight. Before he could react, a cannonball, seemingly shot from nowhere, hurtled toward the wall. The impact unleashed a furious storm of stones, bullets, and arrows, raining down like a fiery hail. Each projectile burst into flames the moment it struck the earth, creating a chain of explosions that lit up the forest floor. The duke turned to flee, but he was trapped—fire and destruction engulfed him from every side.

Out of the inferno, as if born from the flames themselves, a figure emerged: a girl, her ethereal beauty accentuated by long, flowing white garments. Her hair, light as moonlight, cascaded down to the ground, and vast wings arched from her back. The duke's mind raced, scrambling to remember old tales from his childhood. What was this creature? What name did they give to beings of such power?

Before he could grasp an answer, the girl spoke, her voice soft yet laced with an ancient authority. "Do you love war so much, duke? Then look at it closely. What you see before you is not a vision of my making, but the true memories of those who endured this terror. I once asked the people to give me their memories, and they surrendered them willingly, desperate to forget. For years, I carried the weight of their pain, but I learned that human memory cannot—should not—be erased. Eventually, I set their memories free, releasing them back to their owners. But some of those poor souls had already passed, leaving their memories behind, locked in my caskets. Now, at last, those memories have found a new host."

"But these are not my memories!" the duke cried, recoiling from the vivid, horrific visions surrounding him.

"They are yours now," the girl replied, her voice turning cold and unforgiving. "I am a vila, keeper of the forests, and I command this. You will forget all your schemes, your ambitions, your life before this moment. Instead, you will be haunted by the memories of those who suffered at the hands of men like you. You will see what they saw, feel what they felt—until the end of your days."

With that, the vila unfurled her mighty wings and soared into the sky, her figure vanishing into the sunlight, which now poured generously over the earth below. The forest, untouched, transparent in its purity and so familiar, swayed peacefully, its green waves glistening in the morning light. Two young gnomes sat on the roots of a great oak tree, their eyes wide with joy as they gazed up through the leaves, watching fragments of sky shift and dance in the gaps between branches. They knew that no matter where they might wander, all they needed to do was look up at the sky through the leaves, and the magic of the forest would reach out to them, enfolding them in its boundless, eternal happiness.

A Tale of the Garden City

"MILOŠ, YOU'RE FINALLY HERE!" A thin voice echoed from an overgrown hollow at the foot of a low hill. Rushing down the path, Miloš bent down by the shallow stream, carefully slipping his hand under a snag. At that very moment, he felt a cold sensation on his palm and gently brought the tiny rain elf into the light. The elf, fluttering anxiously around him, chided him reproachfully:

"Well, where have you been for so long? Too busy with your love life?"

"You're too young to talk about this," Miloš admonished sternly.

"Be that as it may, you have completely abandoned us," the elf continued, not the least bit embarrassed. "Look at what's happening around us!"

Miloš understood what the elf meant. From the outside, the forest seemed unchanged—lush with greenery, a kingdom of inexhaustible power. However, upon closer inspection, it was evident that all living things were parched with thirst. The spreading branches, once generous with shade, now barely shielded the dry soil beneath them, which had already begun to crack, sending out thin threads of wrinkles to the very roots of the trees. The air, motionless in the heat, seemed afraid to move, mirroring the forest's stillness.

With his serpentine insight, Miloš sensed how life was subtly ebbing from the greenery around him, down to the smallest atoms. He had noticed this back in his village, sensing the thirst emanating from the pale yellow fields of wheat and barley. That was why he had come here today, understanding what he had to do.

"I know, serpents have always been lovers of beautiful girls, and you have no equal in this," the elf continued, his voice ringing with indignation. "But your main task is to protect our region, to care for the crops and all living beings. In the past, serpents often had to fight dragons. Now, thankfully, there are no dragons left, and all you have to do is to make it rain on time! On time! But with your turbulent love life, it feels like we're in for a real drought. My new house, by the way, is drying up before my eyes!"

"Don't panic," Miloš interrupted. "That's exactly why I'm here."

With these words, he took a deep breath, hoping to absorb the scents of the world around him. The forest responded with a dizzying mix of aromas, seasoned with a lung-scratching dryness. At such moments, Miloš felt as if all living beings were drawn to him by invisible threads, which wove into his body, sprouting like plant seeds. These invisible shoots, blossoming, drew juices from him, at the same time infusing him with their amazingly potent energy.

Miloš felt his blood, boiling with primordial force, begin to course through his veins faster, as if liquid fire, hot like volcanic lava, were mixed with it. His true, deep nature, no longer contained within the fragile walls of his human form, finally broke through, scattering the remnants of his skin. In its place, scales as hard as steel began to grow, and with each new cell, an unearthly strength surged through his body. This power flowed into him with every gust of wind, with the slightest movement of air, penetrating through his pores, filling his veins with uncontrollable streams of life.

Miloš breathed in this life with his entire being, merging with it until he felt an absolute inseparability, as if down to the smallest atom he consisted of the sun's heat pouring from above and the groundwater bubbling deep below. The energy of heaven and earth, reaching its zenith, erupted from him with a desperate cry. At the same time, the scales on his back parted, revealing webbed wings that unfurled like those of a dragon.

There was perhaps no greater happiness in his life than experiencing this mystical moment over and over—the moment of his rebirth. Reborn anew each time, he entered the world renewed, cleansed of everything artificial, external, and superficial. At that moment, there remained in him only one naked essence: the indomitable power of the fusion of elements, the pristine integrity of a living being. Drawn by the feeling of absolute unity with everything around him, he spread his wings and soared upward toward the mountain peaks on the horizon.

At first, the earth seemed reluctant to let him go. It stretched endlessly ahead with mountain slopes and rocky ridges blocking his path. Yet, Miloš did not give up. He stubbornly gained altitude, clashing with the air currents and absorbing them completely. The forests, which had just begun to recede, rushed toward him again, parting as if wanting to pull him into their impenetrable thicket.

As he approached the steep slope, Miloš sharply ascended with such force that it seemed he intended to crash into the sun's disk. The rocks, which had just appeared as whitish veins on a flat forested carpet, grew larger before his eyes, rising and blocking the sun. They scattered into ledges and crevices, solar slabs and sharp shadows, growing into the sky and tearing it open with their sharp contours. They seemed inextricably sewn into its flawless blue, as if it was on their granite shoulders that the heavenly stronghold rested.

Miloš knew from experience that this was just an illusion. No matter how unattainable the peak might seem from below, and no matter how endless the mountains appeared, all he had to do was exert a little more effort, rush upward more sharply, overcoming the flow of air beating against his chest. The rocky ridge hanging over him would sink, fall down, and helplessly diminish, torn from the sky and thrown at his feet in a motley carpet. Wrinkled and pierced by ribbons of roads and rivers, the earth slipped away, replaced by air transparent in its purity. He was surrounded by this air, and the young serpent unmistakably sensed the first premonition of moisture in the streams of heat entangling him.

Spreading his wings, he hovered above the ground, slowly gliding over the mountain peaks. Each scale opened and bristled as if trying to absorb all the moisture from the air. Like a tiny bird flung into the frighteningly endless sky, Miloš felt a familiar thrill, comparable only to the purest child's prayer. He froze before the infinity surrounding him, silently pleading on behalf of his entire people, of that little world to which his kin belonged. A child of earth and sky, of the human race and magical creatures, he modestly asked some incomprehensible power for rain.

As if in response to his unspoken request, clouds began to gather, casting bizarre shadows on the ground below. They slid down lazily, as if hesitating, then, swaying with a sigh, their heavy sides began to intertwine, drawing in the heavenly blue. The premonition of saving moisture grew more acute, permeating Miloš from within, and his entire serpentine nature rejoiced at the approach of rain. A distant rumble warned of its arrival, and Miloš slowly descended to the ground, respectfully giving way to the elements he had summoned.

Lightning flashed across the sky, illuminating his scaly back, and the first crystal-clear drop burst from the swollen clouds. Tiny though it was, Miloš felt it immediately—not with his body, but with his whole being. Following this drop, another, and a third rushed to the ground, and within minutes the rain was lashing his back, filling his wings with streams of water. In delight, Miloš bathed in them, choking on them as he had once done with air currents. He could not drink his fill, like the parched earth, thirsting for healing water.

When Miloš reached the ground, all living beings were already rejoicing, filled with vitality, and ringing like the blows of powerful water jets on leaves dusty from drought. Washed and renewed, the forest blossomed. The rain elves, performing incredible pirouettes in the air, penetrated into the very core of the water jets and rushed along with them, laughing like children. In these rare moments, they forgot their anxieties and completely surrendered to the joy of flying, intoxicated by such a rare feeling of security.

The flower elves, on the contrary, feared the heavy rains and hurried to take refuge under the canopies of their blossoms. But even they, clinging to the wet, strong stems, felt how they came to life from within, sharing in the joy of renewal. A squirrel coquettishly peeked out of its hollow, badgers and hares scampered into their burrows, birds hid, but Miloš felt that they were all just waiting for the rain to end so they could, with joyful hubbub, dancing, and singing, announce to all living things the end of the drought.

At such moments, Miloš felt a special sweetness from being the protector of all living things. There was no arrogance or patronage in this, only the pleasant burden of responsibility and satisfaction from the results of his work. The main reward this feeling gave was the sense of involvement in others' happiness. Having contributed to their joy, Miloš recklessly surrendered to it as if he were a little elf who had just escaped mortal danger. The joy of co-creation connected him to everything around him and, shared with the whole world, immediately multiplied many times, merging in a single stream of jubilation.

Miloš was so immersed in this feeling that he did not immediately notice an unpleasant chill. Streams of rain flowed unceremoniously down his collar, and his thoroughly wet hair stuck to his forehead. With a start, he realized that he had automatically turned back into a human without noticing it.

"Come here, poor fellow!" he heard a low, slightly grumbling voice. A gray-bearded gnome looked out from a small niche in the rock and motioned for him to take shelter. Miloš ran to him and saw a whole family of dwarves caught in the rain in the midst of their work. The forest hard workers had been building new caves in the rock and now waited impatiently to continue their exciting activity.

"Well, you created quite the weather!" the gnome continued to grumble, glancing at the wall of rain that cut off the exit from the niche.

"Yeah, I went a little too far," Miloš laughed cheerfully.

He suddenly felt a pang of sadness because he could not share this fascinating world with those dear to him, including his parents. Unlike him, they were ordinary people and could not see elves or dwarves. Only the vilas—forest fairies—sometimes appeared to people, opening the door to an invisible and beautiful world. Miloš knew that his father, Goran, was himself the son of a vila, but for some unknown reason, the magical gene, due to some unknown whim of nature, was passed on not to the son, but to the grandson of the fairy.

Miloš did not know his grandmother, though he heard from his father that she died tragically many years ago. However, he felt his extraordinary abilities even before he learned the story of his origin. Miloš was very young when, while visiting his uncle Rado, he saw an elf circling over a flower bed in his garden.

"Uncle, who is this?" he asked in amazement, but no matter how hard he tried, Rado could not see anything.

The world in all its diversity opened up to Miloš from an early age. In winter, he saw snowflakes cheerfully whispering among themselves, weaving a single carpet and carefully covering the ground. He felt life everywhere—in the water and the wind, in the whisper of the grass, and even in the slight winking of the rag dolls sitting on the fence at the entrance to the village tavern. Sometimes Miloš saw golden streams of time stretching from earth to sky, dissolving into an incomprehensible eternity. And he always knew how to predict rain long before it started, catching the smallest hints of moisture in the air—a happy premonition of renewal.

Miloš could dissolve completely into the nature around him, yet sooner or later, he would begin to yearn for human companionship. At times, he was angry at the invisible creator who had placed him on the edge between the human world and the realm of magical creatures that inhabited the earth. Belonging equally to both worlds, Miloš sometimes felt his difference from others in both of them, often at the most inopportune moments—especially in matters of the heart.

The little elf might mock his adventures, but he had no idea that Miloš was deeply unhappy. Ancient beliefs held true—no woman could resist the spell of the serpent. Girls would fall in love with Miloš without any effort on his part, throwing themselves at him, and upon rejection, would suffer bitterly over their irreparable loss. At first, he enjoyed this trait, relishing the quick victories, but soon, he grew weary of it.

Like all young men, Miloš dreamed of true love—tender and reverent, emerging slowly in a delicate interweaving of feelings, in the joy of mutual recognition, in the innocent simplicity of the first intimate connections, not yet of bodies but of souls. He longed to see a girl's heart open to him, not because of his magical powers, but from an impulse known only to her. He wanted to win his chosen one gradually, touch by touch, in the silent game of first caresses, afraid deep down of rejection, never knowing the outcome in advance.

But alas, all the love in his life was predictable, and thus, dull. Not long ago, Miloš had broken up with his latest passion, Jovana, who, predictably, fell in love with him at first sight. Her passion initially inspired him, but soon, it gave way to the usual disappointment. No miracle occurred. From the greedy sparkle in her eyes, from the intensity of her responses, from the empty platitudes she spoke, he realized she had not fallen in love with him, Miloš, but with the serpent—unearthly beautiful and brave, harboring the hidden power of a winged guardian.

The thought of Jovana scratched unpleasantly at Miloš once again, but there was nothing to be done. He still had to return to his native village. The rain had subsided somewhat, and only timid drops still caressed the leaves, waiting for a stray movement to shake them to the ground in a swift stream. Miloš walked along the path, hearing the trees rustle gratefully behind him, and the birds, emerging from their hiding places, joyfully sang of the wonders of distant lands from which they had returned in the spring.

* * *

Approaching his home, Miloš noticed strangers sitting in his yard from afar. They were dressed unusually richly for the village, and the patterns on their caftans were unlike anything he had seen before. Blue and sea-green, they combined in bizarre iridescences that involuntarily attracted the eye. Their curls resembled foaming waves, and their golden buttons resembled pearls in sea shells.

"Probably more guests here to try our cheeses," Miloš thought. His mother, Danka, had made the best cheese in the village since her youth, and over time, her fame spread so far that even guests from neighboring principalities often visited to try her culinary delights. However, these visitors seemed to have come from distant seas. Seeing Miloš, they immediately stood up and, waiting for him to catch up, respectfully addressed him:

"We have heard that you are among the last of the serpents on earth, the guardian of forests and fields, the master of rain," began the uninvited guests with a florid tone.

"Not a master; I merely call upon the rain to save my land from drought," Miloš tried to correct them, but they paid no attention.

"We are envoys of the sea king Leander, and we have journeyed from the ocean depths, for we have heard that no woman can resist your charms," the guests continued. Miloš froze in bewilderment, struggling to comprehend how such a reason had driven these strangers to traverse such great distances in search of him. Despite all his adventures, he had never encountered girls from the ocean depths, and had scarcely ventured beyond a few neighboring villages.

"A terrible misfortune has befallen our land," the envoys of the sea king continued. "A cunning vampire has taken up residence among us. Unlike his ancestors, he does not feed on the blood of his victims, but on their deepest loves and joys."

"But how does he do this?" Miloš asked in confusion.

"By gaining his victims' trust, the vampire is allowed to enter their souls," the guests explained. "They reveal to him the world that brings them the greatest joy, and the vampire convinces them to share this world with him. Descending into the very depths of another's heart, the vampire unerringly senses where his victim draws the most strength, what gives them happiness, and what is most precious to them in the world around them. Once he identifies this, he begins to slowly siphon the life force directly from the center of their joy. It is as if he connects with the surrounding world through the person who loves it, and, having connected, he drains the life from it with all his vampiric bloodthirstiness."

"But doesn't the victim feel what he is doing?" Miloš was surprised, feeling noble anger boiling within him towards the insidious monster.

"The tragedy is that for a long time, the victim feels nothing," the visitors nodded mournfully. "The vampire knows how to replace another's love and happiness with his poison brilliantly. He permeates everything dear to his victim with it, and the victim may not notice the substitution for quite some time. It seems to her that she is still drawing from the source of her joy, not realizing that in reality she is becoming more and more attached to the vampire, absorbing new doses of his poison."

"And what happens then?" Miloš asked, holding his breath.

"Then the vampire vanishes," the envoys of the sea king replied. "He disappears as if he had never existed, and only then does the victim discover that everything she once loved has become faceless and dead. Both she and everything around her are saturated with vampire poison. Everything that once brought joy now causes only pain. It is as if the vampire steals from people their very ability to be happy, leaving behind only a crippled, empty shell."

The speaker fell silent before adding with effort, "The daughter of our king, the beautiful Anita, has also fallen victim to this vampire. None of the beauty of our underwater domains can bring even a faint smile to her face anymore. On the contrary, everything that once gave her strength and formed the foundation of her life now only disgusts her. She says that the world she once loved no longer belongs to her but to the vampire. He took it with him, leaving Anita only faceless reminders of the grief that befell her, poisoned with venom."

"You want me to fight this vampire?" Miloš asked, feeling a strange mixture of excited anticipation and anxiety before what would be his first real battle.

"Alas, that is hardly possible," the servants of the sea king responded gravely. "Princess Anita's elder brother, the fearless sea knight Uldis, has already ventured forth to battle the vampire, but he has not returned. It seems that no one can defeat this vampire. But that is not why we have come to you."

"Then why?" Miloš asked, his curiosity piqued.

"We have heard that women cannot resist the charms of serpents," one of the visitors repeated stubbornly. "The beautiful Anita has lost the ability to love. Nothing and no one in the world can bring her joy anymore. Human abilities are powerless here, but perhaps your magical power can work a miracle. We want Anita to fall in love with you, and through that, the ability to love will return to her."

"But if I cannot reciprocate her feelings, the heart of the unfortunate Anita will be broken again," Miloš warned.

"Yes, but those wounds can be healed," the guests countered. "You won't try to permeate her whole life, and you don't possess a terrible poison that replaces joy with pain. If Anita once again feels a thrill and desire in her heart, it will already mean that she has been healed."

Miloš pondered the weight of the words he had just heard. The gift he had come to view as a curse could indeed work wonders for this unfortunate girl. His ability to instantly evoke love—an ability he had grown to dread like a contagion—might now serve as a balm, a remedy.

"But what if I fail to awaken her love?" he questioned, a secret hope stirring within him. Could it be that he might finally encounter a woman who, unlike all the others, would not fall instantly and inexplicably in love with him without really knowing and understanding him, and therefore not loving him truly?

"Very well, I will try to help you," he resolved.

"The journey to the sea is long," his visitors replied. "Of course, if you could turn into a serpent, and we could, say, fly upon you..." They fell silent, their eyes expectant. Miloš smiled knowingly and began to explain that he could not transform into a serpent at will. Such a transformation was only possible when it was necessary to protect other creatures. Besides, no one had ever flown on a serpent before. With a sigh of disappointment, the sea king's servants began their trek back, guiding Miloš toward their oceanic realm.

The day turned to night, and predictably, a new dawn broke. The travelers paused in towns and villages along their path, and Miloš marveled at the changing landscapes. The further they journeyed from his native places, the more the villages resembled small towns. Neat and dotted mostly with stone houses, they occasionally featured wooden balconies or cornices over the roofs. Even the streets here, like in a city, were paved with cobblestones. Each village radiated peace and comfort, with short, winding streets that playfully meandered down hills and disappeared between the houses, emerging again on the approaches to the tall stone churches. Each miniature, homely town seemed to beckon, promising happiness and serenity to travelers.

" Everything in this world is capable of bringing joy," Miloš mused, looking around. "How did it come to be that a single vampire could strip all living things of their beauty in the eyes of his victims?"

Gradually, the streets of new towns and villages grew more spacious, and the stone from which the houses were built became larger and lighter. Under the rays of the hot southern sun, the buildings appeared almost white, gleaming in their brightness. The paving stones of the streets grew smoother as if polished by the ceaseless movement of sea waves. At last, the winding line of the beach and the masts of ships piercing the sky came into view.

"Well, here we are!" proclaimed the sea king's envoys. In an instant, they somersaulted through the air and transformed into beautiful dolphins. Describing symmetrical arcs above his head, they disappeared into the sea's depths, leaving playful ripples that distorted the contours of the ocean floor and lapped gently at Miloš's feet. He stood on the shore, feeling the moisture-laden air seep under his skin, awakening a primordial sense of strength in his blood.

Miloš realized that he could now transform into a serpent if he wished. He unmistakably recognized the growing energy within, poised to burst forth in all its might. Yet, an unusual timidity seized him. Not daring to trespass without invitation, Miloš stood humbly on the shore, watching as the ripples gradually faded and the water's surface smoothed. Through the clear water, the corals and every sand-dusted shell became increasingly visible.

Suddenly, the surface of the water swayed once more, and the waves hurried to Miloš's feet. The sea trembled and parted, releasing from its depths a slender female figure. She seemed to be entirely made of water which mysteriously merged into her perfect forms. Miloš couldn't discern whether she walked or floated on the waves. The sea carried her as if birthing her before his eyes, crafting and honing every curve of her body with its waves. Then, it parted before the beauty of its creation, carefully spreading out at her feet, inviting her to the land.

A girl, as beautiful as a mermaid, with hair tinged with blue and eyes the color of the sea's depths, stood before Miloš. It took the young serpent a moment to look into those eyes, and he involuntarily stepped back, encountering a cold wall of indifference. It wasn't that every woman had fallen in love with Miloš before. If a girl didn't interest him, he knew how to restrain his charms. But even in such cases, the glances of women he met expressed at least curiosity and interest.

Never had he encountered such cold, unfeigned indifference. There was no arrogance or ostentatious contempt, which often masks resentment. There was no hint of feeling—any feeling. The gaze of the sea princess was as deep as it was empty, absolutely empty, as if all life had been burned out of it. Her face was like a flawless painting or sculpture, almost indistinguishable from a person, except for its complete lifelessness. Not a single spark, not a single movement flashed in her eyes; not a single, even the most fleeting shadow touched her face.

The dolphins, poking their heads out of the waves, watched this scene with bated breath. Realizing Miloš's powerlessness before the magic spell, they dove back in disappointment, waving their tails in farewell.

"You shouldn't have wasted your time and made such a long journey," the girl said guiltily, turning to Miloš. "I asked my father not to send his servants to earth and not to disturb anyone."

"You didn't disturb me at all!" Miloš began to object hotly. "I was glad to make such a journey to see you."

"Don't work so hard on it," Anita smiled weakly. "You see that it doesn't help."

Work? The word cut Miloš unpleasantly. Never before had communicating with a woman caused him difficulty. What he said to Anita was absolutely sincere, but it didn't work.

"I am sure that this will pass," he tried to cheer her up. "I am simply not the kind of person who is capable of causing any feeling in you, and that is right—I am not worth it. But I am convinced that sooner or later someone or something will appear capable of melting your heart."

"If you saw how beautiful the world in which I lived was, how deeply and selflessly I loved it, you would understand that there is not and cannot be anything better in the world," the princess objected bitterly. "But even it does not touch me anymore. Everything around me seems to have died, and only repulses me. Sometimes I want to run away from here, but the trouble is that I have nowhere to run, and nothing else is capable of causing joy either..."

"But you have nothing to do with it," she immediately interrupted herself. "You are capable of experiencing love, and this is wonderful. Enjoy, rejoice, live, appreciate every moment of your happiness. You can't even imagine yet how huge it is."

She said this sincerely, Miloš didn't doubt it one bit. But amazingly, even with this sincerity, her eyes expressed absolutely nothing. It seemed that some inattentive creator forgot to put the last, but so necessary, detail into this unearthly creation—a living heart.

"You don't need to run anywhere from here," Miloš firmly stated. "I will find the damned vampire and take from him the life force that he took from you and from what is dear to you. What surrounds you now will soon shine with new colors. Believe me, I can handle him."

"I didn't ask you to fight the vampire," Anita began fearfully.

"You don't need to ask me about it," Miloš assured her. "Just tell me where I can find this monster."

"No one except his victims has ever been able to see the vampire," the sea princess began to dissuade him. "He appears to each of us in a new form, and it is completely impossible to fight him. My brother, Uldis, tried to do this, and since then I have not seen him."

"Your brother was not a serpent," Miloš objected. "If there are no dragons in my lifetime, a vampire will be enough for me. Just tell me where he might live."

* * *

The road to the vampire's castle was long and arduous. Miloš traversed countless mountains and rivers until he reached a towering, barren rock, piercing the sky. Stepping back, he focused all his strength, transforming once more into a mighty serpent. This time, he did not do this to protect his village or to merge with the elements and plead for the needs of the earth's inhabitants. He did it for the one he could not forget, despite the cold indifference with which she had met him.

The thought of the sea princess inspired Miloš, and he felt the familiar, primordial energy boiling within him, demanding release. His eyes narrowed momentarily before widening, flashing with fire. Strong, membranous wings unfurled behind him, and Miloš, pushing off from the ground, soared toward the distant point where the rocky peak met the sky.

Upon reaching the summit, Miloš was surprised to find himself on a broad mountain plateau. Contrary to his expectations of a cold, gloomy crypt, a beautiful garden city spread out before him. It seemed as if all the joy of the earth, stolen by the vampire from his victims, had been gathered in this corner of paradise.

In the wondrous garden, small towers and palaces were nestled, bearing no resemblance to Gothic gloom. Built of cheerful red brick, they were framed with blue rims adorned with whitish curls of patterns, reminiscent of clouds in the sky. The same motifs decorated the facades above the windows, and the palace roofs were covered with bright yellow tiles, as if painted by the sun itself. The carved stucco, the welcoming green shutters, invitingly wide open—all these features filled Miloš with a childlike joy. This long-forgotten feeling of serenity washed over him, making it difficult to remember why he had come to this place.

"I see you've settled well, feeding on others' joy!" Miloš shouted into the void. "But now it's time to return everything you took to its rightful owners!"

"Am I against this?" came a mocking voice, echoing from all directions. "Everything you seek is here, just go and take it."

Miloš searched in vain for the source of the mysterious voice. Only the sun shone around, reflecting off the yellow roofs and bluish windows. The feeling of celebration engulfed him again.

Pure, untainted joy emanated from every corner of the garden city. Perhaps this was how paradise should look: shining, jubilant, woven from happiness, and permeated with serenity. Spreading palms playfully touched the palace walls, overgrown bushes entangled their bases, and this harmony of nature and man-made beauty merged into a single feeling of tranquility.

Struggling to stay alert, Miloš entered the open door of one of the red towers. Instead of a building, he found himself on the shore of a lake. The area was overgrown and wild, but this only added to its romance. Below, at an abandoned pier, boats huddled together. "Lovers must have spent their best days here," Miloš guessed. The essence of someone else's happiness lingered in the air, filling this secluded corner with warmth. It took Miloš some time to find a path out of the overgrown nook. He emerged once more into the jubilant, shining garden city.

Miloš boldly entered its towers and palaces, each revealing more magnificent scenes. Exotic islands, tempting with hidden secrets; a burning strip of sunset over the sea, seeming to scorch the sky and leave fiery trails on the water; the light of lanterns, scattering pearls on the snow—these visions not only surrounded him but also radiated human warmth. Each scene bore the imprints of a soul, and now they grew from it, as from the most fertile soil in the world.

Every time Miloš encountered someone's memory within the palace walls, he returned to the garden city. With each return, it seemed lighter, airier, and more vibrant. All the beauties of the earth, warmed by the ardor of human hearts, were gathered here. Miloš wondered why one vampire needed so many manifestations of happiness. How could his cold heart contain all this embodied love, scattered over cities, villages, castles, temples, natural wonders, and simple huts?

Here, thundering waterfalls opened up before him, and modest forest paths spread out. There were memories of those who cherished sailing in a boat along a sunny path at sunset, marveling at how its stern cut through the molten gold of the sun's rays dancing on the water. For others, happiness was embodied in a small overgrown courtyard with a creaky swing, which, though not very tall, once gave an unforgettable feeling of flight in childhood. Each of these small worlds drew him in, each imbued with comfort and warmed by someone else's memory, perfect in its own way. And above all this splendor, like an invisible shell, rose the garden city—the vampire's endless domain.

Miloš searched for the memories of the sea princess for a long time. Finally, entering one of the palaces, he saw the room take on bizarre outlines, distorted by the swaying of the waves. It felt like an underwater grotto. Flickering light surrounded him, making the space seem to expand and contract, changing color and shape constantly. Emerging from the cave, Miloš found himself among riotous, multicolored coral reefs. He marveled at their intricate interweaving, which encompassed all the shades of the sky and the earth. Stepping carefully on them, as if on scattered jewels, Miloš ventured deeper into the underwater kingdom. With each step, new depths opened before him.

Everything swayed with the movement of the waves, distorted in the bizarrely refracted light, beckoning him through the dense water. Different shades of blue, light blue, greenish, and violet reigned here, flowing into one another and trembling in the flickering reflections. Stunned by this incomprehensible beauty, Miloš plunged further, unable to tear himself away. Suddenly, he saw the sea princess before him. Here, in her familiar world, she was especially beautiful.

"I must tell her that no one can steal this incredible beauty," thought Miloš, without taking his eyes off her. "The underwater world is not frozen like a painting. It continues to live, change, and rebirth itself every second. Even if the vampire took away her love for this world at some point, these corals, underwater rocks, and schools of fish can evoke her love again. Life does not stand still. I must tell the princess that she, too, is changing, and together with this world, they can rediscover and love each other, healing the wounds of the past and giving birth to new life forces in each other."

The discovery seemed so simple that Miloš was amazed it had not occurred to him before. "You will be able to love your world again, I am sure of it," he said, taking a step towards her.

"But I never stopped loving it," she answered in surprise, looking up at him.

Miloš was confused. In this strange, magical world, he was met by a different, past Anita, who had not yet experienced the terrible loss.

"But this is not her, this is just a memory of her," flashed through his mind. Yet, when the princess smiled, the disturbing thought vanished, melted by the warmth of her smile. The feeling of happiness finally overwhelmed Miloš, and he succumbed to it, dissolving in the first true love of his life.

"Wonderful," whispered the vampire, watching through a large crystal ball in his gloomy, night-black living room. "This boy will forever be stuck in the remnants of other people's memories and images of what people once loved. Like the sea prince Uldis, he will never find his way back now," the vampire said, laughing triumphantly.

* * *

The days dragged on, dreary and monotonous. Miloš did not appear, and with each new hour of his absence, his mother Danka's anxiety grew. Rumors that her son had not simply gone to help the unfortunate princess but had decided to fight incarnate evil did not reach her immediately. When Danka learned of this, a chilling horror seized her mother's heart. Her husband Goran tried not to show his concern, but it was clear that he, too, could not find peace, worrying about their son.

"We need to turn to your aunt vila," Danka finally suggested to her husband. "If something happened to our son, only she can help find him."

Goran did not object. He himself understood that being a human, he would not be able to help the fearless serpent, whose life now lay somewhere beyond the boundaries of the human world he was accustomed to. The forest fairies, as the only bridge between people and magical creatures, remained his last hope. He and Danka ventured into the forest together, a place that seemed equally welcoming to everyone but did not reveal itself to everyone in its entirety. Vila was already waiting for them as if she knew in advance that Miloš's parents would sooner or later turn to her for help.

"He is not here," she told them with unfeigned sadness. "Believe me, I myself would give a lot to bring our boy back. But alas, it is beyond my power. Miloš is now too far away, beyond our reach. He is stuck in other people's memories, and he can only be returned together with them. If the one whose favorite places he immersed himself in learns to love them again, if she can return to herself what the vampire took from her, the spell will wear off, and Miloš will be able to return."

"But that is impossible!" Danka cried out in despair. "The servants of the sea king who came to us a few days ago assured us that there was no power on earth capable of returning princess Anita to her former joy. That is why they turned to my son for help. If she could not return her love all this time, then how can she do it now?"

"In that case, we can only hope for a miracle," the vila sighed. "Miloš is determined and strong, but when it comes to love and its loss, another magic is at work, beyond my control. It is too powerful and incomprehensible for all living beings without exception."

"We will go to the sea princess," Goran answered decisively. "I do not know how exactly, but we must help her cope with this, at least for the sake of saving Miloš."

In a span that felt both brief and endless, Goran and Danka reached the jagged line of the coast. The sea greeted them with a majestic calm. It spread out, approaching their feet and lazily teasing them with the foam-dusted crest of the waves, which rolled onto the shore in a gentle rhythm. In the distance, the backs of serene dolphins flashed briefly before diving again into the endless depths. At last, cutting through the almost motionless surface of the water, the figure of the sea princess emerged. She walked towards the uninvited guests, and it seemed as if the sea itself, incarnating in her form, was coming out onto dry land.

Trying to contain their pain, Miloš's parents recounted to Anita what the vila had told them. "If it were within my power to give half my life to save him, I would do it," answered the princess of the ocean depths. "But it is not within my power to do the impossible. How can I love again what was burned out of my soul with a hot iron?" she said into the void, as if still hoping that someone invisible would give her the answer she so desperately sought.

* * *

The sea swayed at her words, responding to every sound of her voice, and colorful schools of fish flew up to the sides like sparks of joyful fireworks. Beauty and delight surrounded Miloš every minute, turning his life into one continuous, undiluted joy. And yet, over time, he began to secretly feel a strange deficiency, an incompleteness of the happiness that filled him. Anita was always friendly and cheerful with him; she looked at him with eyes full of love, and everything that surrounded them was also filled with her love. It took Miloš a while to understand that this absolute love lacked the main thing—movement and renewal.

As if hoping to disprove his suspicion, he tensed all his muscles and tried to feel the familiar fusion with everything around him. Invisible threads were about to reach out to him from every coral, from the smallest shell embedded in the slippery silt, from every playful fish darting around them. Now a primordial force would burst forth from the depths of his being like a fiery stream, and the happiness of rebirth would cover him completely, dissolving him in the raging elements...

However, the only response to his impulse was silence and stillness. Shades of blue and violet, catching the refracted light, swayed around serenely. Suddenly it dawned on Miloš: among the splendor of the sea depths, he had never seen sea or ocean elves. Warmed by love and comfort, the underwater world, nevertheless, remained lifeless, frozen in time. Miloš could not find those creatures he was always able to see. Though he was a serpent, he could no longer turn into a serpent. A terrible realization finally pierced him, and Miloš rushed to the princess.

"Anita, my dear, this is an illusion," he began to implore her. "This world is beautiful, but there is no movement in it, and therefore there is no life. Nothing stands still, and therefore nothing can be returned. To preserve the love for what is dear to us, we must generate new love every minute. It is difficult, but only thanks to this can no one take away from us what we love. Feeling pain, we are ready to give up the old and look for the new, forgetting that what we consider old acquires newness every day. Love can be long and even eternal, only if it is constantly changing and growing. What surrounds us now is not love."

Anita listened to him and only laughed in response to his words. She was the same illusion as everything that surrounded them in this beautiful world. Despairing of reaching her, Miloš pushed off from the bottom and soared upward. He swam, breaking through the water column to the surface, just as, being a serpent, he broke through air currents to the top of a mountain, and from there—to the sun, into the shining, ringingly transparent infinity. The extraordinary beauty of the underwater world, which had recently enchanted him, now seemed to bristle, rising from the bottom as a silty suspension, and then fell upon him. The last jerk, the last movement upward, to the blurry reflection of the solar disk swaying on the water...

Miloš broke free from the water and found himself standing once more in the middle of a sun-drenched garden city. However, the energy of his transformation could no longer be contained. He was becoming a serpent—powerful and merciless—and with every second of this metamorphosis, the beautiful red brick buildings sank, collapsed, and crumbled into fragments of walls adorned with blue borders and white paintings.

The serpent soared above the ruins of the once-lovely garden city and, after circling above the devastation, hurried back to where the real, not illusory, sea stretched out.

He landed on the sand, damp from the recent high tide, and saw his parents, Goran and Danka. Before he could even ask what they were doing there, Miloš suddenly noticed the sea princess. She rushed towards him, unable to hide her joy, and, embracing him, whispered with relief, "You're alive! How glad I am that you returned alive!"

He hugged her back and, looking into her eyes, noticed a gleam of awakening of some new feeling, which immediately resonated with music throughout his entire body. The sea rolled up to their feet, caressing their soles—so majestic, unchanging, and yet completely different from what it had been yesterday. Dolphins still joyfully leaped from its waves, and across the water's surface, from the side of the destroyed vampire castle, the handsome Uldis, the prince of the underwater world, approached. With a smile, he came to the savior of his sister and extended his hand to Miloš, as if inviting him into the depths of the ocean like a dear guest.

The air trembled around them, filled with sea moisture. It pulsed with a constant life, unaffected by evil, and growing through suffering and loss, inevitably proving stronger than death. Driven by love and generating love, it filled the world, being the main force of its rotation and the ultimate secret, beyond even the most powerful magic.

www.ingramcontent.com/pod-product-compliance
Lightning Source LLC
Chambersburg PA
CBHW070423310726
48977CB00003B/819